A king must have

want one...

Though the crown prince of the Benin Kingdom, Crown Prince Osad Edoni, is prophesied to marry a local girl, Eki Alile, he refuses to meet her. He finds the whole idea ludicrous and has already decided on a different destiny that he would do anything to see through.

However, it seems fate brings them together when Osad picks Eki to be his temporary queen, a pawn in his game plan to marry his true love. Eki has no choice, and nothing left to lose.

Will they ever fulfil the prophecy, or will Osad cheat fate?

Dear Readers,

I am excited to share with you the story of Eki and Osad. I hope that you enjoy reading it as much as I enjoyed writing it.

Although I have always considered myself a storyteller, I never thought I had the patience to settle down and write a novel, especially a fictional one. I played around with the story in my head for many months, and even after I started writing, I had to rewrite many parts of the book before I was satisfied that the story on paper resembled the one in my heart that I wanted to share. It is a beautiful story, and there are so many lessons to take away.

By popular demand, I am working on a new story. Although it is not a follow on from this one, it will feature some of the characters from this story.

I would love to hear your thoughts about this piece and what you would like to see in the next novel. Please write to me through my website, eturuvieerebor.com, or via my email eturuvie@eturuvieerebor.com.

I look forward to hearing from you.

Evie.

For Hadassah

Special thanks to Linda Ijomah and Godwin
Eghianruwa

PROLOGUE

Two years ago

Unbelievable!

Yes, that is what it was. Unbelievable! Shocking!

Had she heard him right?

Did he really say those things about her?

The crown prince had some nerve. Who did he think he was?

The crown prince of the Benin Kingdom, that's who.

Even then, surely, it did not give him the right to speak about her the way that he just had. Evidently, he had no desire to marry her, and the feeling was mutual, but to speak of her with such disdain was unacceptable.

It began as a funny story, this talk of her marrying the crown prince, or so Eki Alile thought. A year ago, the chief priest of the Benin Kingdom, Chief Amadin Isekhure, had visited Eki's father. Eki's father, Chief Zogie Alile, was a palace chief and friendly with the chief priest who was the head of all palace chiefs and the most fearsome and revered chief in the kingdom. Understandably so as he was the mouthpiece of the gods and his word was law. Well, shortly after he arrived, Eki's mother had asked Eki to serve refreshments to her father and his guest. She had reluctantly agreed as she was the only child at home at the time, and she did not want to get into another fight with her mother. Eki hated household chores of any kind.

As far as she was concerned, there were people paid to do such work, and though her family was not wealthy, she knew her parents could afford a maid and failed to understand why she had to be forced to clean and cook and carry out other mundane housework. Her mother always said they didn't need a maid and that girls in a family needed to learn to take care of the chores as they required the skills to be good homemakers. Eki never understood that concept, and she thought it was archaic. She told her mother at every chance she got that she would never marry a man who expected her to clean and slave over a hot stove. She had not attained her law degree to wither away as a man's maid. If he wanted a maid, he could marry one. Her boyfriend, Odaro Ezomo, was the son of an extremely wealthy Benin chief and their house was crawling with maids who did all the domestic chores from cooking to cleaning and shopping. So far, she was on the right path; Odaro would not expect his wife to be without maids. Her mother, however, thought that no man worth his salt would marry a woman who was useless at taking care of the home and expected maids to do everything. This had been a bone of contention between Eki and her mother for years, and naturally, she was not her mother's favourite child.

On the day in question, Eki obediently took a tray with refreshments to the living room where her father sat with his guest. She had never met Chief Amadin Isekhure before, although the locals discussed him a great deal. Eki took no interest in the monarch, the palace, or the chiefs who worked closely with the king. When she had entered with the tray, an unusual and utterly unconventional event occurred. Chief Isekhure had instantly risen to his feet. Eki thought it was odd; he was an elder and a chief; he should not rise upon her entry. He stood silently; his eyes were boring into her as she approached. Eki had been so nervous she had just about dropped the tray. Her father, who knew how careless and clumsy she could be, had leapt to his feet and taken the tray from her, setting it down on the coffee table.

"You may go. We will serve ourselves," he had said dismissively, flashing her a disapproving look.

Eki bowed her head to the chief priest by way of greeting, but as she turned to leave the room, his words had caused her to stop.

"I feel extremely privileged to have met you, at last, Your Majesty."

Was he talking to her? she wondered as she spun around to look at him. She wasn't the only one stunned; even her father was staring at their guest with incredulity.

"I have seen your face in countless dreams. You

are the queen of this kingdom." His voice conveyed assurance. He turned to her father. "Have you ever taken her to see His Majesty?"

His Majesty was none other than *Omo N'Oba N'Edo Uku-akpolokpolo,* Oba Idahosa Edoni of the Benin Kingdom. The king had recently lost his queen, the beautiful and formidable Queen Esohe, and many speculated that he would never marry again.

Chief Alile shook his head. "None of my children has been to the palace or met the king," he answered.

Chief Amadin Isekhure nodded his head. While many chiefs were notorious for taking their daughters to the palace in the hopes that the king would select them as a wife or concubine, others preferred to keep their daughters far away.

Chief Alile had three daughters, and Eki was the last of them. She did not speculate as to her father's reasoning in keeping them from the palace. Still, if she were to hazard a guess, she would say her father did not want to place his daughters in a polygamous situation, which was highly probable in the palace as the king could marry as many wives as his enormous wealth allowed. Her father had, however, paraded his daughters before many wealthy men in Benin.

For as long as Eki could remember, they had lived an average life; theirs was a lower-middle-class family, and her father was never without plans to advance his status. First, it had been to bag a chieftaincy title, which had helped somewhat. In recent years when his daughters reached marriageable age, the plan was to marry them into prominent Benin families and gain for himself wealthy in-laws who would bail him out of imminent poverty.

The first person he had attempted to marry off into a wealthy family was Aisosa or Aiai as she was fondly called, first by Eki and then everyone else in the family. Aiai was the oldest of his three daughters; she was seven years older than Eki and six years older than Eseosa, who was eleven months older than Eki. Aiai had rejected a wealthy suitor and given her virginity to her boyfriend Efe Inneh to force her parents into consenting to their desire to marry.

"Take her to see His Majesty at once. She is our queen," the chief priest stated, causing Eki's heart to increase in its pace.

Now, the problem was Chief Isekhure did not say more than that and conceivably because he did not know more than that. Nonetheless, Eki's father had been unable to take her to the palace as swiftly as he wanted to because Eki had deliberately delayed the trip as long as she could. Subsequently, Chief Isekhure died. His son, Usi Isekhure, living and working in America returned to Benin to assume his father's position as chief priest of the kingdom. When Eki and her father did go to the palace, they met with Chief Usi Isekhure, who directly prevented the king from touching Eki in any way.

"She is the queen. My father was right," said the younger Isekhure. "But, my lord, she is not your queen. She belongs to another king."

"Another king?" Oba Edoni had asked, frowning

in confusion.

"Yes. She is reserved for the crown prince, my lord," he clarified.

And so, it began.

Eki spent a lot of time at the palace and in the company of Oba Edoni who took it upon himself to teach her the culture of the Benin people. Not that she was unaware of the culture, she was a Benin woman, and the daughter of a palace chief and her father had taught the culture to her himself. With Oba Edoni, however, she was learning what it meant not just to be a Benin woman but to be the Benin queen. He had great faith in the words of both chief priests, but Eki had her doubts, or maybe it was that she had no desire to be married to some prince whom she had never met. Besides, she had a boyfriend and a life planned for herself that was utterly opposite to what the rigid life of a queen would be. She had not told Oba Edoni that she would not marry his son. She had not seen the point. As far as she was concerned, the crown prince was the one to do the asking, and if he proposed to her, she would reject him, and that would be the end of it.

Earlier today, Oba Edoni had called her to say that he was sending a car to pick her because the crown prince was in the palace and he wanted them to meet finally. As Eki rode to the palace, she was both anxious and terrified. Although she had no desire to marry the crown prince, the new chief priest had said that Eki and the prince would fall in love at first sight. So far, they were yet to meet, but falling in love, at first sight, didn't look plausible in the slightest. At least, not from her point of view.

They were worlds apart. The crown prince was from the wealthiest family in the kingdom and was set to inherit not only his father's throne but his business empire, which was worth billions of dollars. Plus, if there was any truth in what she'd heard, the prince's business empirc was already as big as his father's. There was, additionally, the fact that he had spent most of his life abroad and had received the best western education that money could buy. By contrast, Eki was from a lower-middle-class family and had never been abroad. She had studied locally and had recently completed a degree in law from the local university and passed her bar exams.

Before today, there had been two attempts by Oba Edoni to get Eki and the crown prince to meet, but on both occasions, *Mr-high-and-mighty*, as she liked to think of him, had refused. She had gone to the palace on Oba Edoni's instructions, but the crown prince had failed to turn up, with the explanation that he was busy at his palace and unable to make the trip to the Oba's palace to meet with Eki. As he was abroad most of the time overseeing his and his father's business investments, the opportunities for them to meet had been infrequent.

This was the third attempt, and since the third time's a charm, Eki was confident they would meet, and she was both excited and terrified. If Chief Isekhure was right, and they fell in love, where did that leave her and Odaro? They had dated for years, and Eki had always hoped that they would marry. If she fell in love with the crown prince, then what? It was one thing to decline the marriage proposal of a man you did not love, but once you loved him, saying no was out of the question.

She was driven to the south wing of the palace where the houses of the king and queen were situated. Eki loved the palace, and no matter how many times she visited, she was never tired of gazing upon its beauty and extravagance. It was a vast estate initially built in the pre-colonial era on a massive 700,000 square feet. Its sheer size always caused her to gasp, especially when she compared it with her father's modest four-bedroom two-bathroom duplex built on a mere 5,000 square feet. The royal palace was comprised of four wings, each having its entrance to the estate. Eki had been given a tour numerous times, and she knew that the south wing accessed by the south gate consisted of the king and queen's residences. They were identical semi-detached buildings sharing a garden, swimming pool, tennis court, and gym. The north wing housed the offices of the king and queen, the throne room, state banquet rooms, a massive courtyard, and the palace hospital. As the Royal Palace of the Oba of Benin was at the heart of the conservation and commemoration of the rich Benin culture, the north wing also featured a museum and library; both continuously attracted historians, curators, and archaeologists.

In the west wing, there were ten stately guest houses for visiting VIPs, and the harem, an enormous house built to accommodate no less than a dozen women. It was in the harem that the king's concubines lived. The east wing housed the palace kitchen, the staff quarters, and the garage where all the royal vehicles were parked. The palace grounds were intricately woven with walkways and beautified by plush lawns and exquisite gardens. Within the buildings were scores of hallways and secret passages named after past kings of Benin, and they connected the four wings of the massive citadel. Eki often wondered how the servants were able to find their way without getting lost.

The driver pulled up outside the king's imposing mansion. A white Bugatti was parked on the drive, and Eki guessed it belonged to the crown prince. A guard approached the Audi A8 she had travelled in and helped her climb out of the vehicle. She covered the short distance to the grand double doors bearing the royal sceptres of the Ada and Eben, her high heeled shoes clicking against the stone-paved driveway. The head of the king's personal servants, known as the omuadas, opened the door and ushered her inside. He informed her that the king and crown prince were in a meeting and would be joining her shortly. He requested that she wait in the very formal and intimidating Oba Olua Sitting Hall, after which he disappeared.

Eki did not need to be shown around; she knew this house like she knew the back of her hand, having spent countless hours here with Oba Edoni. The servants knew her well, and as she was treated like a daughter, the protocol was always relaxed, and she came and went in the house without restrictions. Eki stood in the grand passage for a while, trying to calm her nerves. As she did, she glanced up at the portraits of the past kings of Benin hanging on both walls of the magnificent hallway and not for the first time did she ponder why they all looked so stern.

"Cheer up," she muttered as she sauntered down the hall in the direction of the reception room.

As she walked past the king's home office, she heard voices. As the door was slightly open, she decided to poke her head around and say a quick hello. She approached, her heels sinking into the thick, luxurious carpet eliminating any sound. She extended her hand to push the door, but her hand froze.

Was that her name she had heard?

The Edaiken of Uselu and Crown Prince of the Benin Kingdom, Prince Osadolor Edoni, sat in the vintage leather armchair across the desk from his father, the Oba of Benin, and zoned out. This talk of some local girl being his wife was becoming old. He thought that after two refusals to meet with the girl, his father would give up the matchmaking game he was playing. Apparently, he was wrong.

He had flown into Benin this morning to discuss some urgent business matters and was due to fly out in only a few hours. He had barely sat down when he was informed that the girl was coming to the palace to meet with him. The last thing on his mind was meeting a woman, especially one that he had categorically said he had no intention of meeting.

Osad drummed his fingers impatiently on his thigh even as he maintained eye contact with his father. Only he, in the kingdom, could look the king in the eye. It was one of the perks that came with being an only son and heir without a spare.

"Dad, we have been through this innumerable times," he spoke abruptly, interrupting the old king. "When I am ready to settle down, I will pick a wife for myself. I know the rules; she must be a Benin woman. I will pick a Benin woman, but I will pick one who, like me, has been educated in the west, a woman who can be my equal mentally and can hold her own amongst my business associates and friends. I certainly won't be marrying some village girl who can't string together enough words to form a coherent sentence in English to the saving of her life!"

Osad was no stranger to the Benin culture. He had been learning it since he was in diapers. He would be Oba of the Benin Kingdom someday, and as such, he could only marry a Benin woman as his heir needed to be full Benin; an heir who was half Benin would never do. His father had encountered a similar problem and had succumbed to his father's will and married Osad's mother. Fortunately, they had come to love each other and had been true soulmates until his mother died a little over a year ago, leaving his father devastated.

Doubtless, his father had it easy. Following a conspiracy between his paternal grandfather, Oba

Ezoti, and his maternal grandfather, Chief Aifuwa-Morgan, his mother had moved into his father's bachelor pad after his father turned forty and was not showing any signs of taking the plunge. While his father had been displeased with the arrangement, he could not resist sleeping with his betrothed. Soon, she was pregnant with their first child Ivie, his father was smitten, and they were married according to the Benin native law and customs. End of story. His father had told Osad many times that marriage to his mother had been the best decision he had ever made. They had not only come to love each other deeply but had had five beautiful children, Osad and his four sisters. He had hoped that Osad would enjoy the same good fortune, but Osad had his doubts.

Oba Edoni looked at his son long and hard, as not for the first time he was reminded of himself as a young man having a similar conversation with his father. Then he threw his head back and laughed.

"Can't string together words to form a coherent sentence," he repeated. "Is this your opinion of the young woman?" He didn't wait for an answer. "And if I may ask, how have you reached such a conclusion on a woman you are yet to meet?"

Osad shifted uncomfortably in his chair. The truth was he was judging Eki based on a stereotype, but he would die before he admitted that aloud. All his life, he had believed that the children of the poor, those who are unable to afford western education, were inferior and not adequately educated.

"How I arrived at such a conclusion is irrelevant. What is relevant is that you are wasting the poor girl's time. I will not marry a local Benin woman. If you want a Benin woman for me, I will pick one who is western educated. That is my final answer on the subject. Hopefully, on this occasion, I have disabused your mind of any possibility that I could see reason in the future regarding this matter. My answer today is no; tomorrow and forever, my answer will be no!"

"You know, she is stunning. I doubt that you will be able to resist her beauty. The prophecy is that you will both fall in love at first sight."

This time, it was Osad who laughed. "I will not be falling in love with a pretty face who has nothing between her ears. Unlike most men, a woman's beauty must be matched with brains to catch my attention."

"And you think her beauty is not matched with brains?" Oba Edoni enquired.

"Well, if she's allowed you to talk her into coming here today, it can't be," Osad said. "Having refused to meet her twice so far, a woman with brains and class would have known not to come here today."

Oba Edoni was quiet for a while and had a faraway look in his eyes. Osad wondered what was going on in his mind. He didn't have to wonder for too long.

"You can't run away from your destiny, Osadolor," he spoke gently. "Indeed, none of us can."

"I agree with you, Father," Osad responded

without breaking eye contact with his father. "And if you believe the words you have uttered, you will stop pushing this ridiculous agenda. Two people who are destined to be together will find each other without anyone's help. You've been obsessed with my love life for too long. It is time for you to find a new interest."

Oba Edoni picked the clear glass paperweight sitting on his desk and threw it at Osad playfully. Osad caught it expertly, and both men laughed.

"Scallywag!" Oba Edoni said, calling Osad by the one nickname he would never outgrow.

Unbelievable and unacceptable!

Eki looked at her reflection in the mirror of the guest bathroom. She wanted to scream in frustration, but this was not the place. She drew in deep cleansing breaths as she willed her heart to stop racing and regained control of herself. She could not afford to show any sign that she had overheard the crown prince voice his prejudiced thoughts of her. He was the future king, the son of the current king, and she was duty-bound to respect his position even if not the man.

She returned to the sitting hall, and it wasn't long before Oba Edoni joined her, alone. Once again, she had been stood up by the crown prince. He had to be the most discourteous person she knew.

"Your Majesty. Good evening, sir," she curtsied.

Oba Edoni's smile brightened the room and lifted Eki's spirit. She loved this man so much. For months, he had been a father figure, mentor, friend, and confidant. They had spent quality time together, and she had opened up to him in ways she had not opened up to her parents.

"Ekinadoese, my darling child." He held out his arms to her as he approached, and Eki moved closer and embraced him. "*Vbo ye he ovbi' mwen*? How are you today?"

Eki forced a smile as she pulled away and faked a joy that she did not feel. No, not after overhearing what the crown prince had said concerning her.

"I feel wonderful, Your Majesty," she responded. "You sent for me," she added, reminding him of the reason she was here.

His brows furrowed, causing deep folds to appear in his forehead. He walked past her and sat on the impressive cream and gold luxury Italian sofa. He was deep in thought as he patted the seat next to him. She sat beside him, and he turned his head to look at her like a man who was seeing her for the first time.

"Eki, how would you feel about going to the United Kingdom to further your studies?"

CHAPTER ONE

Two weeks ago

"What?" Eki stared at the wedding invitation card in her hand in utter disbelief. "I don't believe it!"

It was a mess. Her family was a mess. Only two weeks ago, and the day before she was due to return from her two-year stay in the UK, Odaro had called her on the phone and broken their engagement.

He broke it off on the phone.

He had not even had the decency to wait one day for her to arrive home.

Now she knew why.

He was marrying her sister, her own sister!

He had impregnated her sister!

Eseosa was two months pregnant, and the couple had opted for a quiet wedding ceremony that weekend.

It all made sense now. Eki had thought it was odd for Odaro to break up with her because it was the same Odaro who before she travelled had asked her to marry him. She had been elated, but common sense had told her that if they were going to be apart for two years, it was best not to take their relationship to the next level and wait to see how they fared while being apart for two years. He had not been willing to wait and had insisted they get engaged, and she had stupidly agreed. While she had been away, she had sensed they were drifting apart. The phone calls became fewer and farther in between as the weeks turned into months, and the months turned into two years. He had travelled abroad on business for his father but never managed to find his way to the UK to visit her.

Then, when she was due to return home, he had called and broken off the engagement on the flimsy excuse that his parents did not think she was a right fit for him. That certainly was true, his parents had never bothered to hide their dislike of Eki and Eki had not failed to conceal her dislike of them. For years, her relationship with Odaro had thrived despite her strained relationship with his parents. Why use them as an excuse to break off their engagement? Now, she knew the truth.

When Odaro broke off their engagement two weeks ago, she was disappointed but not in the least bit surprised. After all, they had been drifting apart the last two years she had been away, and although she had not dated anyone while in the UK, being too busy with her studies, she had gone out on group dates and partied with her friends. How could she not? She had travelled with her two best friends, Amenze Giwa-Amu whom she and her family called Amenze Next Door because Amenze had lived next door to them for as long as Eki could remember.

Eki's other best friend was also her first cousin, Tiyan Alile. Tiyan's dad had been Eki's father's younger brother, but she had lost her parents and older brother in a ghastly motor accident in which she had been the only survivor. She had been 13 years old at the time and had moved in with Eki's father and his family. She and Eki being only two months apart in age had been inseparable. Eki – along with friends and family – affectionately called her Cousin T.

Together with Amenze they had gone through secondary school and university with names like the troublesome trio, the three little pigs, the three blind mice and more recently, the three musketeers. Their friends had said concerning their trio; Eki is the romantic voted most likely to get lost in the pages of a romance novel. Amenze is the realist who tells you what is most likely to happen in the real world once you exit the pages of the romance novel. And if you want the statistics of how many couples fall out of love in the first year of marriage, ask Tiyan.

It was Tiyan who had discovered the truth about Odaro and Eseosa. Only this morning, Odaro's sister, Ede, who was seemingly Eseosa's new best friend had come to the house to visit. As they were sneaking around and having hushed discussions, Tiyan had become suspicious that something was amiss and had slipped into Eseosa's room to look for evidence. She didn't have to look too hard to discover a pile of wedding invitations. She had shown the cards to Amenze, and they had sought out Eseosa and Ede and grilled them for more information. Together, they had come to Eki with their findings, which included the wedding invitation card. So, now Eki knew that the real reason Odaro had broken off with her was not that his parents did not encourage their relationship but because he was involved with Eseosa. He had impregnated Eseosa. It was repulsive.

"How did this happen?" she asked Tiyan, waving the card in her hand. "How did they become involved?"

"Well, from what I learnt, after we travelled, Odaro was lonely and missing you, and Aunty Ayi encouraged Eseosa to keep him company and comfort him." She shrugged.

"Comfort him for what reason? Was he bereaved?" Eki screamed in frustration.

She was sick to the stomach of her mother's meddling and schemes. Ayi Alile had continuously favoured Eseosa because she had been born asthmatic and needed more care and attention than Aiai and Eki who were perfectly healthy babies. Sadly, it had not stopped at giving Eseosa extra care and attention; she had sought continuously to strip Aiai and Eki of what was theirs and pass it to her beloved Eseosa. That had included their clothes, toys, food; whatever Eseosa wanted she got. Even if what she wanted, belonged to one of her sisters.

"Eki, wake up and smell the coffee," Amenze said, keeping her voice even and free of emotion. "Understand what is going on here. There is a prediction that you will marry the crown prince; a man who makes Odaro's wealth seem insignificant. Your mother must have felt that if you were going to marry a wealthier man, Eseosa should have Odaro."

Yes, Amenze Next Door, the realist, had spoken. It made perfect sense, and it was so in keeping with her mother's character of robbing Aiai and Eki to enrich Eseosa. Also, her parents had been scheming forever to get their daughters married into wealthy families. Aiai had refused the wealthy suitors arranged for her, choosing instead to marry her true love, Efe Inneh, fresh out of university. As she had lost her virginity to him and her parents feared she might become pregnant out of wedlock, they had allowed them to marry. No one had supported them, but the last two years while Eki was in the UK, their Architectural firm, Homes for Less, had boomed and they were now developing and selling homes worth millions of dollars.

Efe Inneh was now a multi-millionaire and Eki had benefitted from her brother-in-law's new status. Her parents had not gained as they should, and it was understandable after the way they had treated Efe and Aiai over the years. Personally, Eki was excited for her favourite sister and the brother-in-law she loved like a brother. Aiai had been in the UK a few times to see Eki, and there was no hiding their new status and wealth. On one of those trips, she had even purchased a five-bedroom house in Chislehurst, Kent.

The couple now owned one of the Benin Kingdom's largest homes, a twelve-bedroom mansion situated in a highbrow area for the wealthy. Eki had been in awe when she and the girls had visited the estate on their return. It was an architectural masterpiece and a testament to the architectural geniuses that Aiai and Efe were. Yes, they had done well for themselves, but now her parents were looking for another wealthy son-in-law and had poached on what was Eki's. Why couldn't they get Eseosa, a rich man of her own? Why take Odaro from her? No. this was too much.

I am going to kill her!" Eki said to Amenze.

"Who? Your mum?" Amenze asked in bewilderment.

Eki stormed out of her bedroom, without a response. In doing so, she left Amenze and Tiyan with no option but to chase after her.

"Eseosa!" she screamed as she ran downstairs to

the living room.

"Eki, there is no need to do this. Why don't we return to your bedroom and pack our suitcases? Aiai will be here any minute." Amenze tried to reason with her.

They had been in Eki's room, packing their suitcases in preparation for their celebratory trip. The trip was funded in part by Oba Edoni. He was over the moon that Eki had bagged two master's degrees and graduated with first-class honours in both. Efe Inneh funded the other part. He thought the girls had all worked incredibly hard and wanted to give them a good time. Aiai was going with the trio to Dubai, Paris, and London. She was due to pick them up any minute as they would be spending the night in her home before leaving for the airport the following morning.

They had planned the trip even before their graduation, and initially, they had reluctantly, included Eseosa. They had never felt close to her, and she had always deliberately taken a different path from them, but they reckoned she was their sister and should be part of the trip, especially, as she had never been abroad. Not that it was anyone's fault, seeing as their father could not afford for them to go anywhere. Even so, when Oba Edoni had given Eki money to go abroad two years ago, it had been so much that Eki could have sponsored Eseosa's master's degree programme. She offered to, but Eseosa had scoffed at the offer and told Eki that she did not need her charity. Eki had used that money to fund Tiyan, so she did not have to sell her late father's house and the only inheritance she had received to pay for her MBA.

When Aiai's husband had a big break with his business, Aiai had offered to pay for Eseosa to join the others in the UK and pursue a master's degree, but Eseosa had declined, again. At the time, it had seemed stupid, but now Eki knew it was because Eseosa was involved with Odaro. She probably feared that if she left him, she would lose him. As for her refusal to join them on this trip, why not? She was planning to marry Odaro this weekend when they would be in Dubai. It seemed everything had been hushed so Odaro and Eseosa could marry quietly and be in the Maldives enjoying their honeymoon by the time Eki and the others returned from their holiday. Unfortunately, the cat was out of the bag, their parents were out of the house, Eseosa had only one friend with her in the house, so killing her and burying her would be nice and easy.

Eki halted at the bottom of the staircase and spun to glare at Amenze and Tiyan.

"Call Aiai and tell her that we are far from being packed," she barked at Amenze as she entered the living room.

Eseosa was sitting in the living room's dining area looking at a bridal hair brochure with Ede when Eki stormed into the room. From Eseosa's body language, Eki could tell that she was bracing herself for what was to come. She appeared to be looking at bridal hair and making small talk with her future sister-in-law, but she was nervous, that much was clear. She knew Tiyan and Amenze had left her to go and tell Eki everything they had discovered. She had heard Eki call out her name in rage from the top of the stairs. She was no fool; she knew she was about to be swallowed up whole.

Eki ignored Ede Ezomo who was sitting there looking like the cat that ate the canary. No doubt she was thrilled that her brother would not be marrying Eki after all. In the period Eki had dated Odaro she had met Ede on three occasions when Ede who lived in America was visiting her parents and brother in Benin. Eki had not taken to her in the slightest. Ede was a nasty piece of work. Eki was convinced that she would get on famously with Eseosa, another nasty piece of work. Ede had seemed to be competing with Eki for Odaro's affections, and one time when they had both been going out with Odaro, Ede had jumped in the front seat of the car beside her brother and ordered Eki to sit behind. Eki had shrugged it off. If Odaro said nothing about it, why should she? She was so glad that she was through with Odaro and would have no dealings with Ede in the future. She would rejoice later, right now, she had to confront her thief of a sister.

"You are dead!" Eki yelled at her and slapped her twice across the face in quick successions.

Eseosa jumped off the chair and backed away, looking like a frightened rabbit. Ede played the role of a doting sister-in-law and moved in front of her, shielding her.

"Eki, stop this at once!" she shrieked.

Whoever made her Eseosa's spokeswoman? Eki wondered.

Tiyan stepped in front of Eki and moved Ede out of the way.

"Stay out of this, Ede. It's an Alile family matter," Tiyan said through clenched teeth before turning to Eki. "Go on, Eki, rough Eseosa up a little. And allow it, Eseosa, you brought this on yourself."

"What's going on here?" Aiai asked from the doorway.

They had been so engrossed in the scuffle that they hadn't noticed her entrance.

Amenze walked towards Aiai, giving her a brief version of the story. She held out the invitation card, and Eki heard Aiai gasp as she read it. Enraged once more, Eki moved in and slapped Eseosa across the face.

"That is for comforting my fiancé," she announced. "You had no right, you slut."

Before Eseosa reacted, she slapped her again. "That's for getting pregnant." And again, "And that's for conning him into marrying you."

Eseosa screamed and pushed Eki away. "Get away from me and stop assaulting me. Do you want me to miscarry?"

"No, I don't want you to miscarry, but I will disfigure your face, so your husband and in-laws don't recognise you when they come to pay your bride price!" Eki went to hit her again, and Aiai stepped in between them forcing Eki to halt in frustration. She grabbed Aiai by the shoulders and shook her.

"Out of my way, Aiai. This is no time to play piggy

in the middle!"

For years, that had been Aiai's role. She played peacemaker and piggy in the middle, especially when it came to Eki and Eseosa. The sisters had always been rivals. Though their mother blamed Aiai who had always seemed to favour Eki, Aiai maintained that she had preferred Eki because their mother had shown a preference for Eseosa from the get-go. That meant that whenever Eki and Eseosa fought, although Aiai played piggy in the middle, she was always in Eki's corner because their mother would automatically be in Eseosa's corner. That's what happened even now.

"*Vbo na khin?* What is going on here?"

No one had noticed Ayi Alile enter the house.

"What is going on is that your top secret is out. We are now aware that Eseosa is pregnant by Odaro and that they are marrying this weekend. Naturally, Eki is not best pleased." Aiai took on her mother.

Ayi did not even try to look remorseful.

"I am not aware that Eki has ownership rights over Odaro Ezomo forbidding him from marrying any woman of his choice."

"Mother!" Aiai was shocked. "How can you say a thing like that? For five years, Odaro visited this house to court Eki, and Eki only!"

"For the last two of those five years, Eki was not here, and his interests switched to Eseosa. As he was not married to Eki, I saw no problem with that, and I see no reason to explain myself or my decision to any of you."

"I don't believe this!" Aiai said.

"Believe what you like. But one thing I must tell you is that I will no longer condone you causing problems in my home, Aisosa. Please leave. Go to your husband's house. Isn't his new mansion big enough for you?"

Aiai held her hands up in defeat. "I rest my case." She began to move in the direction of the front door.

"Ladies, I am waiting outside in the car. Get your

bags, and let's leave." She looked at Eseosa. "Have a good wedding and a good marriage." Her eyes wished her anything but.

She reached the door and then changed her mind and spun around.

"You know what? I have one more thing to say before I rest my case." She looked at Ayi. "You have no shame, Mother. I remember that it was only last year when I came here to warn your *ashawo* of a daughter to stay away from my husband and my marital home."

She looked from Tiyan, and Amenze to Eki, all of whom stared back at her in shock. This was news to them because Aiai had never mentioned it. She went on.

"On one of my trips to the UK to visit you, this *azen* we call a sister visited my marital home in the middle of the night straight from a party, drunk as a skunk and dressed like a whore. She attempted to seduce my husband. Fortunately for me, he didn't cave, and when I returned, he told me the story and showed me the security footage. I came here to warn Eseosa, and ask my mother to keep her wretched daughter in her home, and do you know what she said to me? She said, well, Aisosa, if your new-found wealth has entered your head and you are jetting all over the world and leaving your husband at home, you can't blame anyone but yourself if another woman seduces him. If it is not Eseosa, it will be someone else."

Aiai paused. Tears filled her eyes as she addressed Ayi once again.

"I am ashamed to call you, my mother. I am going to my husband's house as you have advised. Your daughter now has a husband, he better be enough for her, because if I catch her anywhere around my marital home or my husband, I will shave her head."

She proceeded to leave the house but not before giving Eseosa a look filled with disgust. "*Azen*!"

The room was quiet after she left, but Ayi soon broke the silence by turning on Amenze and Tiyan. She gave them both a nasty look.

"*Vbo khin?* Why are you lingering? Do you also have something you want to get off your chests? Do you not have a trip to make?" she quizzed furiously.

Tiyan and Amenze mumbled and grumbled as they sluggishly left the room to go upstairs and finish packing their suitcases.

Ede stood to one corner with an arm around Eseosa's shoulder in solidarity. Not that Eseosa needed any extra. She had enough camaraderie from her mother, and God knew they were both cut from the same cloth because, like Ayi, she did not even have the decency to look embarrassed.

Eki shook her head and turned to her mother. "When will you stop your scheming, Mother? When will you stop robbing Aiai and me to pay Eseosa? You urged Eseosa to go after Odaro, and while she was at it, you encouraged her to make a move on Aiai's husband. What were you hoping to gain? And have you no sense of decency?"

"You watch how you speak to me, young lady! Another insolent word from that foul mouth of yours and I will slap your face," she shouted.

"I pray that you do it!" Eki raised her voice to match Ayi's. "Aiai is not here to play piggy in the middle, and I am in no mood to honour a woman who has failed to act as a mother in my twenty-four years of existence. Think about that before you raise your hand. I have had enough of you and your evil schemes. You constantly nagged me about keeping my virginity. If I even went out for a drink with Odaro, when I returned you wanted to know if I was still a virgin. You tormented Aiai and me, lecturing us of the importance of going to our husbands as virgins. Yet, here you are, marrying off your choice daughter, at two months pregnant. What will your church members and fellow Christian mothers think, I wonder?"

She turned and began to walk away.

"What they think is none of your business!" Ayi snapped. "*Gha khian!*"

"You are such a hypocrite, Mother!" Eki shouted in disgust. "A hypocrite!"

She stormed upstairs to her bedroom, desiring to get away from her mother and sister. She was appreciative of this trip and even more pleased that when she returned, Eseosa would no longer be living at home. It was good riddance to bad rubbish.

As she packed her suitcase in a frenzy, she vowed to pull an Eseosa on her parents. If they thought it was okay for Eseosa to get pregnant while unmarried, she was going to get pregnant too. When she returned from this trip, she would not be a virgin, and hopefully, she would be pregnant to the shame of her parents. It would be a great way to kill two birds with one stone. Embarrass her parents and ensure she would never have to marry the proud peacock that was the Benin Kingdom's crown prince.

Later that evening, Eki called at the palace to see Oba Edoni. She wanted to see him before she travelled and to thank him for funding part of the trip. He noticed she looked unhappy and asked what the matter was. Soon she was reliving the day's events and telling him all that had transpired, leaving nothing out.

"That's okay, dear child. Don't worry about any of it. Let it go," he counselled.

"How can I?" she asked. "He was mine."

"Was he truly yours?" he asked but did not wait for a reply. "If he were genuinely yours, he would not be marrying your sister. Maybe it is time that you focus on aligning yourself to receive what you are meant to have instead of fighting over what you were never intended to have."

CHAPTER TWO

Present-day

Crown Prince Osad Edoni groaned as he opened first one eye and then the other. For a moment he was disoriented as he recalled where he was. It had been the pattern for the last three months. He had travelled a great deal such that whenever he woke up, it took him a while to recognise his surroundings. Tonight, he was sleeping in his king-size bed in the large Manhattan penthouse he had acquired a few years ago and currently called home. It was spread across two floors and 10,000 square feet and was a stunning apartment featuring five bedrooms and six baths, a double-height living room, outdoor terraces, and a private rooftop swimming pool. It was the perfect bachelor pad.

He looked at the smart digital bedside clock. It was 1:00 am. He had been asleep for less than an hour. He groaned again as he eyed his phone which had woken him up as though willing it to be motionless. No such luck; it continued to vibrate and grate on his nerves.

"This had better be important," he muttered under his breath as he leaned over, flipped the switch of the table lamp, and grabbed the annoying device.

He took one look at the screen and inhaled sharply. The caller was none other than Chief Usi Isekhure. Without any doubt, he was calling from Benin. It had to be at least 6:00 am in the kingdom of Benin. Whatever had instigated this call was crucial. Usi Isekhure was not a man who made calls that were not critical or lacked purpose.

At only 28 years of age, Usi Isekhure was the chief priest of the Benin Kingdom and head of the council of palace chiefs. Next to the Oba, he was the most revered man in the Benin Kingdom as he was the mouthpiece of the gods of the land. Usi and Osad had grown up together in America, but more than two years ago Usi's father, Chief Amadin Isekhure, the chief priest had died, and Usi had returned to

Benin to assume the office of the chief priest which was hereditary. Like all the chief priests, his forebears, who had preceded him, Usi had an unusual gift of predicting the future.

Some friends in America had referred to Usi as psychic, and this ability had made him an extremely wealthy man. Before returning to Benin, he had been a stockbroker and amassed a vast fortune not only for himself and his clients but also for friends who bought and sold shares when Usi did. Although they were close and Usi was like the younger brother Osad did not have, they had rarely seen and spoken to each other in the almost three years that Usi had taken up the chief priest's office. The primary reason being that like his father before him, Usi believed that Osad was meant to marry the local beauty, Eki Alile and as Osad was vehemently against that idea he had actively avoided Usi.

Besides, Usi had become the Oba's right-hand man like his father before him. In that role, he was too busy to entertain Osad or participate in the shenanigans they had gotten up to in America. If Usi was calling him at 1:00 am, it had to be for one reason only. He braced himself for what was to come even as he answered the phone.

"Isekhure," he said by way of greeting. "Talk to me."

Usi was a man of few very words and wasted no time getting to the crux of the matter.

"The great white chalk is broken," he said matter-of-factly. "*Oba gha to kpèrè. Ise.* Long live the king."

Osad disconnected the call and tossed the phone away from him as though it were on fire. He sat up on the edge of the bed and buried his head in his hands. His father was gone. For a moment, he considered what that meant. Three years ago, his mother had died in his arms, and he was yet to recover. And now *this*; his father, mentor, and friend had left him without any warning.

That was not all. Osad's life was about to change forever. Chief Priest Isekhure had called him king, and so he was. He was now king of the Benin

Kingdom. He was no longer Edaiken of Uselu and Crown Prince of the Benin Kingdom. No. He was now the Oba of Benin, the monarch of the sky reigning on the land, and a host of other titles by which the Benin people called their Oba. This was what he had waited for and been prepared for all his life. Now it was here. Was he ready? He was anything but ready to fill his father's shoes, but that was irrelevant. The shoes had become vacant, and he had been raised to fill them and so fill them he must.

He got to his feet and began to pace the dimly lit room. A million thoughts were racing through his head all at once. He had to return to Benin immediately. The death of the king would not be officially announced until he was in Benin. He would be making the announcement himself. He would also need to tell his sisters privately. All four of them were living in London now.

Although they had all been raised in their father's home in Houston, Texas, his oldest sister, Ivie had married a Benin man living in London and relocated.

Eventually her three unmarried sisters, Ewere, Omo and Orobosa moved to London and now they were all married and resided there. Orobosa had been the last to relocate to London, and her relocation had been forced to keep her apart from his best friend, Edosa. Edosa Aihie was a man that Osad highly respected. He was a high-level palace chief and a kingmaker. He had held this position following the death of his father twenty-one years ago when he was only ten years old.

Both men had been raised in the same Benin community in Houston and had only fallen out when Osad had learnt of Edosa's interest in Orobosa. Edosa had been so in love he had been willing to give up his friendship with Osad. Not even when Osad and Ivie conspired to separate the couple by sending Orobosa to London did Edosa give up. He was a multi-millionaire tech Wizkid and could run his business from anywhere, so he had packed his bags and moved there, too.

The couple had sought and received the king's

blessing, and Osad accepted that they loved each other and wanted to be together. They had been happily married for the last six months. Osad often wished he had what they had, but his business gave him no time to develop a relationship with a woman he was interested in. Not that he had been interested in any woman for a long time.

He would need to pass through London and break the news to his sisters before flying to Benin. It would not do to tell them over the phone or for them to call their father and worry because he was inaccessible, worse still for a PA or chief of staff to answer the phone and speak in a way that aroused suspicion. No, that would never do. The pain would be too great, and to ease it somewhat, it was imperative that he broke the news to them himself and be available to comfort them. He had to be on the move.

He picked up his phone from the corner where he'd thrown it. Straightaway he called Sato Ihaza, who apart from his housekeeper, Mrs Odia, was the only staff who lived with him in his penthouse. Sato was ex-US Army and for the last four years had served Osad in the capacity of a driver, personal assistant, and head of security. They had only just returned together from a trip to Houston where Osad had been attending a board meeting at a company where his father was a significant shareholder. He guessed Sato would be asleep and hated to rouse him, but they had a trip to make before dawn, and this conversation could not wait. He dialled the number, and Sato answered on the first ring. Osad rolled his eyes. Did the man ever sleep?

"Sato. Meet me in my office in five." He hung up and walked into the bathroom to splash water on his face. There went his hopes of having a goodnight's sleep.

When Osad strolled into his home office, dressed in a pair of navy pyjamas bottoms, and a navy lounge tee-shirt, he found Sato standing in the middle of the room.

Osad wasted no time getting down to business. "The great white chalk is broken," he stated pausing at the doorway and waiting a moment for the words to sink in.

There was a flash of emotion on Sato's face, and he opened his mouth, to offer his condolences to Osad and shut it again as the full implication of the words and what they meant hit him. He was standing before the king. Unexpectedly, and before Osad stopped him, he bowed his head and knees in reverence.

"*Oba gha to kpèré. Ise.* Long live the king."

Osad sighed. He had heard those words countless times, but they had always been directed at his father. Today, they were directed at him. Once more, he questioned whether he was ready for his new life.

"Sato, please rise. Officially, I am not yet king." Osad walked into the office and sat behind his desk.

Sato rose with a look of confusion. "But, Your Majesty," he began.

"And talk like that will reveal the current happenings to the world before an official announcement is made. For now, I remain Your Highness and will be addressed as such. Sato, my sisters do not even know what has transpired. You call me Your Majesty once in front of them, and the news is out."

"I understand, Your Highness."

Osad rolled his eyes. "What is the matter with you? I thought we agreed that you only address me as Your Highness in public?"

"I know, but things have changed. Now, you are the king."

Osad studied him briefly and sighed. "You are right. Things have changed, but I am still Osad to you in private."

"Okay." He nodded.

"Now, sit down. We need to plan our trip."

"Shall I make us some coffee?" Sato asked.

"That's a good idea. Lace mine with brandy." He

needed to stay awake and deaden his senses.

While Sato made the coffee, he called Chief Usi Isekhure and quizzed him thoroughly on the king's passing. The king had died in his sleep and was discovered by his chief servant who had gone to wake him. He had summoned a palace doctor and Chief Isekhure. The doctor proclaimed the king had suffered a mild heart attack in his sleep. Osad did not need to tell Chief Isekhure what to do; nevertheless, he ordered that the palace be sealed, and the news remain top secret until he arrived. He was going to round up the call when Usi broached the issue of Eki Alile.

"Now that you will be returning to Benin for your coronation, it is time you consider meeting Chief Alile's daughter. You are king, and you need a queen."

Osad groaned. Not this matter again. Not this girl again. Couldn't he be left in peace to mourn his father? Well, there was too much to do right now even to contemplate mourning his father. He would have neither the time nor space to grieve his father until after his coronation, if at all—what a mess.

"Remember to whom you speak, Isekhure," Osad began in a warning tone. "You do not tell me what to do." On that note, he hung up.

"Usi giving you trouble?" Sato asked with a smile as he handed him the coffee.

Sato knew that while Osad loved Usi like a little brother, Usi also grated on Osad's nerves and Osad was not averse to letting him have it whether by lashing out with his mouth or with his fist. For anyone who didn't know them the level of formality between both men gave away none of the closeness and fondness that existed between them.

Osad smiled, and at that moment, his love for the younger man was evident. "He's a fool," he muttered, and Sato chuckled.

"I hope that you haven't unpacked because we leave for London in a few hours. We will spend the night and fly to Benin. Where is Sky King now?"

Sky King was a brand-new Bombardier Jet, and the latest addition to the fleet of private jets Osad owned jointly with his father. He used it whenever he travelled outside the US on business. It was ideal for long haul flights.

"Incidentally, Sky King is in London as we speak. Your father had sent the crew there on an assignment, and they are due to leave tomorrow."

"Call the pilot and let him know we are on our way and that I will be flying Sky King to Benin. I don't need to tell you that the king's death is top secret as of now. Contact the pilot on the ground and ask him to get the jet here fuelled and ready to leave for London in four hours. Call London and arrange with the head housekeeper at the house in Belgravia. I won't be staying there but the crew will. Check me into The Dorchester using my Alias Owen Morgan. You will be staying with me. I would prefer not to have any other security detail. I do not wish to call attention to myself, and especially not on this trip."

"How do I look?" Eki asked from the doorway of the master bedroom of Aiai's home. "Good enough to eat?"

She twirled and waited for her sister's comment. *It had better be good,* she thought. She had spent more than an hour preparing for her outing. Tonight, she was dressed as her alter ego, Mystery, created during her days as a postgraduate student in the UK. Initially, she had created Mystery for Halloween and costume parties only but seeing her black leather pants and halter neck blouse, in the closet of the room she used in Aiai's home, she decided to go out tonight dressed as Mystery. It was the night she intended to lose her virginity, why not add a little enigma to the mix to create some excitement? So, she donned the leather pants that fit like a glove and revealed her slim, shapely figure and the halter neck blouse that showed a good portion of her shoulders. She held her hair back in a ponytail made longer by a hair extension that came up to her waist.

Eki did not usually wear makeup, but as Mystery, she wore heavy makeup, especially a black shimmering splatter paint makeup around her eyes that created an eye mask. A smoke grey pair of contact lenses changed the colour of her eyes. It was the perfect disguise. She slid her feet into a pair of stunning court shoes in plush suede, and as summer nights tended to be chilly, Eki completed her outfit with a cashmere fur trim shawl draped over her shoulders. She thought she looked spectacular and was the perfect epitome of mystery, elegance, and above all, seduction.

Aiai tore her eyes up from her laptop and the video call with her husband and three-year-old daughter, Zena, to glance at Eki. She groaned and rolled her eyes.

"Are you even now considering this?" she asked, taking in Eki's attire.

Eki sighed. *Talk about a party pooper*, she thought. Aiai better not talk her out of going ahead with her plan. She was already starting to feel a bit nervous and didn't need to hear talk that would make her chicken out.

"Yes. Otherwise, I would have gone out with Cousin T and Amenze Next Door," she pointed out.

It was the last night of their trip. They had seen Dubai and Paris and were now visiting London. They had stayed in Aiai's UK home situated in Chislehurst Kent, and from there they had seen all the sights of London they had been unable to see while students there. Aiai's home was a dream, a five-bedroom house with a spa and swimming pool; it was to die for. They had thoroughly enjoyed their stay, but all good things come to an end. They were due to return to Benin the following day, and the girls were making the most of their last night.

Amenze and Tiyan had gone on a double date. Amenze's boyfriend, Greek shipping magnate, Dimitris Papadopoulos, whom she had met on the MBA course had taken her to dinner, and as he had his cousin Alexander with him, Tiyan had tagged along. Eki had opted out. She had other plans. Tonight, was the night she had been waiting for and the last thing she wanted was to be with anyone who was going to rain on her parade.

"Darling, please hold while I talk to your crazy sister-in-law," Aiai said to her husband and gave Eki her attention once again. "Okay. So, run this plan of yours by me again."

Eki sighed. How many times would Aiai demand she go over the plan with her? This was becoming old not to mention tiring.

"Aiai, for the last time, it's quite simple. I go to a bar. I have a few drinks, for courage, a charming man invites me to go home with him. Pop, my virginity's gone like a balloon along with our parent's hope that I will one day be queen. *Capiche?*"

"Text an address, so we know where to pick up your dead body. You know just in case your virginity's not the only thing you end up losing before the night's over."

"Not funny, Aiai," Eki called over her shoulder as

she exited the room.

An hour later, she sat in The Bar at The Dorchester sipping a cocktail named *The Notorious Kiss*. She was a little tense, as she had no idea how this night would turn out, but she felt reckless. Tonight, she was going to do a deed she would regret. Before this night she had done numerous things, she lamented, but none had been deliberate. Tonight, everything she did would be intentional.

Eki was bent on hurting her parents as much as they had hurt her. She would show them, she seethed. She was going to pull an Eseosa on the family, and they'd better not lecture her about it. What was sauce for the goose was sauce for the gander, after all. Furthermore, losing her virginity and getting pregnant would undoubtedly mess up their plans of becoming the Oba's in-laws as the crown prince would only marry a virgin.

CHAPTER THREE

It was 10:00 pm when Prince Osad strode into The Bar at The Dorchester Hotel wearing a slight frown. He was unsure why he had come. If he wanted a drink badly, there was a minibar in his suite and what wasn't offered was obtainable via room service. He had only just checked in and intended to go to bed, but for incomprehensible reasons, he had fled his room, not desiring to be alone a moment longer.

A lot had happened in the last sixteen hours since he received the news of his father's demise, and he appreciated that his life would never be the same again. He had arrived in London three hours ago and had gone straight to his father's London home situated in Belgravia. Sato had arranged for his sisters to meet him there for dinner after which he had broken the news.

Thankfully, Sato had also requested the presence of their husbands or Osad would have had the challenging task of calming and comforting four wailing women. Good thing they had not been in public because all decorum had been thrown out the window. His sisters had not behaved like the princesses they were born and raised to be. Not that anyone could blame them. Their dad had been exceptional and would be missed.

Osad had let their husbands comfort them while he looked on and accepted once again what was now his reality. As they regained their composure, they realised the full implication of the news and that their new king was seated in the room and swiftly, they were bowing, and curtsying and Osad had to put up a hand asking them to stop. Was this going to be his life now? People constantly bowing before him and unsure how to act in his presence?

That was not all. This morning, journeying to JFK airport where his jet was waiting, he suddenly realised he had no idea when he would be returning or how he would handle his business concerns going forward. Delegation was not his thing. It had been his father's, and his father had delegated all his business responsibilities to him. For the last seven years ever since he was twenty-five, he had run his father's vast business empire at home and abroad with his father relinquishing more and more control to him as the years went by. Now he had a kingdom to run as well; there would be no time for the journeys he frequently made. He would have to learn to delegate more responsibilities to the numerous vice presidents that spanned the various departments of the international conglomerate.

A new day had dawned for Osad. He was king, and there was no going back. He sighed. It came with great responsibility, great sacrifice. He could no longer live his life as he saw fit, but according to the dictates of his people, the Benin people. He was expected to return straight away for his coronation ceremony during which he was expected to marry.

His people would need a queen as much as they needed a king. He did not mind; he was thirty-two and overdue, the only problem was he had been so busy with his business that he did not have a woman in his life now let alone a woman who fit the criteria. And if there was one time, he felt lonely, and in need of a spouse, it was tonight.

He felt empty and exhausted. He had lost his father who was coincidentally his best friend, and as if that were not bad enough, he was stepping out of familiar terrain into the unknown. He had been preparing to be king all his life, but what did he really know about leading people? One thing was sure; he could never be his father. His father had been a great man, a king loved and admired by his people. Osad knew he was not half the man his father had been, and there lay his greatest fear.

If only he had the right woman with him, the right woman for him, one who would fit into his life perfectly like she was made for him and this journey. With the right woman, he was confident he would succeed. The million-dollar question however was, where did he begin to find the right woman?

He halted in his tracks for a split second as he

observed the woman sitting at the bar. He had been lost in his thoughts that he had not noticed her initially. For the first time since leaving his room, Osad knew why he had come out. He wanted her. He wasn't sure if it was for the night or longer although truth be told, he didn't do one-night-stands.

Moreover, he hadn't planned to have a woman in his bed tonight. Once he set eyes on her, though, he was determined not to leave the bar without her. He was not even sure why he was drawn to her, but he knew some extraordinary force, was pulling him towards her like metal to a magnet.

Was that a mask she wore around her eyes or was it makeup? he pondered.

Whatever it was, he found it intriguing, and the mask wearer in him discovered a kindred spirit in her. As a teenager, the pressure of expectations, especially the expectation to act responsibly, had driven him to create an alter ego, Anonymous. Behind that mask, and disguised under that identity, he had been as reckless as any teenager with raging hormones. His father had learned of his activities and had an excruciatingly long conversation with him. Anonymous had been laid to rest only to be resurrected for Halloween and costume parties. In recent years, he was more inclined to act responsibly and on the odd occasion that he desired to act irresponsibly, he used his alias Owen Morgan.

As she sipped her drink, he took the time to check her out. She was built as he liked his women to be. He took a wild guess looking at her long slim legs that she was about five foot and nine inches tall. He eyed her slender frame clad in leather pants and a halter neck blouse. She had the body of an athlete, the perfect body for an athlete such as he was. He wondered how reckless she was willing to be tonight.

Eki was on her fourth cocktail when she lifted her head and saw him approach, the tall, dark, and handsome stranger, who looked like he had stepped off the cover of GQ Magazine. Now, that was her type of man. If only he didn't look so severe. What was his deal? Eki was a good time girl; she loved to laugh and have fun; her mother was never able to fathom it, not even after being with Eki for twenty-four years. Serious, was the one thing she could not pull off successfully, and she often wished other people would lighten up.

She sipped her cocktail while eyeing the handsome stranger who was making his way to the bar and *her*. She sensed he wasn't from around here. He stood out, instead of blending in. She guessed he was a foreigner, probably African American. Hands buried deep in the pockets of his beige designer chinos, which he paired with a navy slim-fit shirt, he looked and walked tall and proud, like a king, like he owned the place.

Eki instantly thought of Oba Edoni and how he walked even in old age, she was sure that as a young man in his prime, he would have walked like this man who was commanding the room. She took in his clothes and the Burberry sneakers, they looked expensive, and she liked what she saw. He was handsome and overall, a sight for sore eyes. She had always wanted her men to be tall, dark, and gorgeous, and need she mention rich and a good dresser? What woman didn't? Odaro was good-looking, dark, and rich, but he was neither tall nor a good dresser. Eseosa was welcome to him.

"What's a beautiful girl like you doing in a bar all by herself?"

The handsome stranger lowered his tall frame into the seat next to hers and broke into her reverie. He turned his head and ever-so-slowly and deliberately looked her over. He was checking her out, leaving her with no doubt that he desired her, which left her bursting with excitement.

Eki quickly scanned his hands, which were no longer in his pockets, and saw that he wore no wedding band. She smiled. She had found the perfect man to take her virginity.

"I take it that you are alone?" he went on.

He was flirting with her. The signs were all there, from the pickup line to the look, to the tone of his voice. Oh, that voice, though. It had to be the lowest, huskiest voice she had ever heard. And she loved his American accent.

"Who wants to know?" she asked cheekily.

"Owen."

She raised a brow. He shrugged.

"Just Owen."

"Well, Owen… Just Owen…. you may call me Mystery."

Now, it was his turn to raise a brow. She smirked. Yes, two could play that game.

"If I tell you anything more than that I'll have to kill you," she warned with a teasing smile.

He held up both hands in mock surrender.

"I think Mystery will suffice … for now," he drawled, keeping his eyes locked with hers.

Eki looked away. His gaze was too intense for her

to match, even after the four cocktails.

"To answer your question, yes, I am alone."

"Perfect," he smiled, revealing a perfect set of teeth; straight, even, and white as pearls. He must spend a fortune at the dentist. Eki would never understand the average American's obsession with their teeth.

"Can I buy you a drink?" he asked, once again disrupting her musing. His eyes were fixed on her as though she were the only person in the room. Except now, he was not looking at her with desire but with concern. He rose to his feet. "Tell you what, why don't we go up to my room and I can order us some after-dinner coffee? I think you've had enough alcohol for one night, Mystery Lady."

Without another word, he turned to the waiter and settled her bill. Next, he was pulling her out of her chair and draping her shawl around her shoulders. Subsequently, he guided her out of the bar and into the brightly lit foyer, moving towards the bank of elevators. All the time, he had a hand placed firmly and possessively against the small of her back. Eki followed without complaint. Not only because she wanted to be alone with him but also because she realised that he was right, she had had one too many drinks, and a cup of coffee sounded great right about now.

His "room" was not a room at all but a suite, The Dorchester Mayfair Suite. Eki's eyes widened as he let her into the ostentatious space that was his to relish. She had no idea what rooms cost at a hotel like this, but she was confident they were pricey, and a suite was a whole different ball game. You had to be super-rich to afford one of those. She made herself comfortable on the grey fabric sofa while he reached for the phone.

"Would you like to eat?"

Eki shook her head. "I'm not hungry. Thank you."

She listened as he ordered coffee and dessert for two. When he was done, he joined her. To her disappointment, he sat in the armchair facing her, with his legs out front and knees spread, exuding dominance.

"Have you had dinner? Or were you drinking on an empty stomach?" he demanded sounding more like a father scolding a child than a man with romantic interests.

"I have had dinner. I had dinner before I left home."

"Home." He repeated the word like he was hearing it for the first time. "Where is home?" he queried.

Eki sighed, next thing he would be asking for an address so he could take her home like she was some stupid child who had run away in a moment of foolishness, leaving her poor parents frantic with worry.

"Kent," she mumbled, folding her hands across her breasts like a defiant teenager. This was not how she had anticipated this evening, turning out. She was supposed to be the classy, sexy, mysterious, Mystery, and this man had turned her into the less confident, awkward, Eki.

"That's a long way to come," he acknowledged. "Do you come here often?"

Eki sighed. This was quickly becoming a disaster. She started to feel like a child caught with her hand in the cookie jar or worse still a criminal being cross-examined by the prosecution barrister.

"No. I don't come here often. This is my first time," Eki answered in a tone that hopefully indicated she was becoming exasperated with his line of questioning.

That much was true. As a London student, her nose had been buried in her books; she had not explored the city as she would have liked, hence returning for this holiday. She didn't tell him that, though. She didn't think that her American friend cared one way or another.

"I see," he answered, and she wondered what it was that he saw. "And do you usually wear a lot of eye makeup?"

"No, only when I dress as Mystery. I created her about two years ago. She is supposed to be everything that I wish I were, mysterious included. The eye makeup that looks like an eye mask is part of her costume. Her never-leave-home-without-it," she grinned.

She expected him to grin back, but he did not. Apparently, he was unamused by her game.

"Why?" he asked, a little curious.

"Why what?" she feigned ignorance.

"Why did you create the persona?"

She shrugged. "Why not?"

He watched her for a while as he sought to understand what kind of woman she was.

Good luck with that! Eki thought.

"Care to tell me why you are here at The Dorchester? And in some form of disguise? That is apart from drinking virtually to the point of inebriation."

A knock on the door interrupted the conversation, and Eki sighed in relief. He rose to open the door to admit room service. They were served, and for a while, afterwards, he asked no more questions. They made small meaningless talk as they ate their chocolate cake and drank their coffee. Eki should have been glad, but she wasn't. She suspected the handsome stranger was not through with his interrogation. And she was right. He soon brought the small talk to an end and went back to questioning her.

"I ask you again, Mystery Lady, why are you here at The Dorchester?"

Eki wasn't sure what it was about him that made her want to talk. Usually, she would have told him to mind his own business, he was a stranger, and she did not need to answer his questions. Except that she did not feel he was a stranger, which was in itself, strange.

"Well, if you must know, I came here to find a man to take my virginity."

To say that he was not expecting that answer would be an understatement. When she spoke, he had been sipping his coffee and he not only choked but spilt some of the hot liquid on his pants causing him to flee to the bathroom.

Eki sipped her coffee not the least bit perturbed.

"If you can't deal with the answer, don't ask the question," she muttered to herself.

He reappeared a moment later, looking more coordinated but wearing a scowl on his face.

"Care to repeat that?" he asked sharply.

She dropped her cup and rose to her feet. "No, I do not care to repeat that. And I would thank you not to speak to me as though I were some errant child. I am a grown woman. I don't need you or anyone to tell me what to do. For a crazy moment when you walked into the bar, I thought you were the one but obviously, I was wrong. Thank you for looking out for me, but I think it is time I went home. Good night, Owen." She draped her shawl over her shoulders and marched towards the door.

CHAPTER FOUR

Osad reached the door before her and barred it with his body. No woman had ever attempted to walk out on him. And if they had, he would not have stopped them. He had never cared for any woman who was not connected to him by blood. He lived by the philosophy that beautiful women were common, and if a woman wanted out, she should be dismissed immediately and replaced with another.

Mystery was different; she fascinated him, and he did not want her to leave. He wanted to know her and not just the woman standing before him but her double who had created the alter ego. Besides, his being with her felt right. He was relaxed in her presence, and talking to her was easy. He had to keep reminding himself that he had only just met her because it sure didn't feel that way.

He realised he had overdone it with the questions. He had never probed into a woman's activities like that. Well, he had, but only with his mother and sisters, and that was because they had been his responsibility with his father being absent a great deal while they lived in America. He had never felt the same level of obligation towards any woman he had known or dated. They were free to do what they wanted, and if he was not best pleased, he ended the relationship. It was always that simple. He did not meddle in their affairs. Until now. Until this woman. She aroused the protector in him, as though she was his, in all ways.

If she were seeking a man to take her virginity, he could easily be that man. He had wanted when he saw her, although not for a one-night stand, which he had to admit was all she seemed to want. Also, he had had no idea she was a virgin. That complicated matters somewhat, but not enough for him to let her leave.

"How old are you?" he demanded.

He guessed she was over eighteen, but he was taking no chances; he had to know for sure. The last thing he needed was for what happened between them tonight to come back to haunt him. So far, he had been on his best behaviour, keeping himself and his activities away from the prying eyes of the press and not giving the palace PR office any reason for concern.

"Twenty-four," she replied, looking everywhere but at him. He noticed she was nervous and fidgeting with her purse.

"And you've never been with a man?"

She shook her head. "I did have a boyfriend for five years, but we never had sex."

Osad frowned. That was odd. She was a beautiful woman; any red-blooded heterosexual man would give an arm to make her his. He wanted to ask why she had remained a virgin, albeit being in a relationship that long, but he changed his mind. She was already uncomfortable with his probing, and he didn't want to cause her any more discomfort. Besides, what did it matter to him why her boyfriend had never slept with her? The fool's loss was his gain.

Except when he, Osad touched her, she was his, and not for tonight alone. He had to ensure that she understood this.

He placed both hands on her hips and pulled her against him. "You're a beautiful woman, Mystery, and I desire you. You accused me of treating you as a child, and I must let you know that when I look at you, I see only a woman."

As if his words were all the encouragement she sought, she leaned into him and pressed her lips to his. It was a simple, chaste kiss, but once her lips touched his, he opened his mouth and devoured hers. She responded with the same degree of ferocity as she wound her arms around his neck, revelling in the kiss until he broke it off.

"I must warn you that this is a bad idea, and you are playing with fire." His breathing was ragged as he whispered into her ear.

"Maybe I don't care," she muttered in response. "Maybe I like playing with fire. Maybe I want to get burned. Maybe I'm feeling reckless tonight." She pulled his head down and kissed him once more.

He broke off the kiss again. "Or maybe you don't know who you're dealing with," he suggested looking her straight in the eye.

She had no clue who he was or what she was getting herself into. He was not a man who took a woman's virginity and let her go. He had been raised to believe that a woman's virginity was sacred, and a man did not take it unless she was his wife, or he intended to marry her. Also, as a Benin king, such as he now was, when he slept with a woman, no other man could sleep with her. It was considered taboo, and the Benin people believed the gods killed such a man or made him mad. Therefore, sex with her could not be the casual affair she was seeking; it would have to result in marriage. Would she want that?

"Maybe you should leave."

Yes, it was best that she did. If she were not a virgin, he would pander to her wishes and lose himself in the one night of meaningless sex she was undoubtedly seeking. God knew his body craved it.

He had been travelling non-stop the last three months, not sleeping anywhere for more than two nights at a time and in that time, he not been with a woman.

Nonetheless, sex with a virgin was not inconsequential if his upbringing was anything to go by. As prince and now, king, he was expected to marry a virgin. Taking a woman's virginity entailed marriage, and for that reason, he had never slept with one. If he touched this woman tonight, it meant marriage and a whole load of complications that he couldn't even begin to describe.

The rules stipulated she had to be a Benin woman to birth the heir to the throne. Apart from her relocating to Benin, there was the possibility of her ending up as wife number two or wife number one while another woman, a Benin woman gave birth to the heir. It was a crazy and complicated situation, and Osad doubted she was ready for it. He knew he was not; polygamy had not been his father's thing. As Oba, his father could have as many queens as he desired, but he had chosen one woman, and it was only after her death he had opened the harem as he took a few concubines, but never remarried, never had another queen, and never fathered children with another woman. His father had deliberately chosen concubines who were middle-aged, widowed, and mothers. That way, there was no pressure to father a child with any of them.

Osad desired what his father had with his mother, but right now, he doubted he would ever have it. His father had been lucky to fall in love with a Benin woman. He was on the verge of falling in love with this woman who, if her accent was any indication, was British and from Africa or the Caribbean. Marrying her would mean changing the rules, and that would be challenging as technically he was not yet king. And to be king, he had to be married, and to a Benin woman. Furthermore, there was the messy business with the daughter of Chief Alile, which undoubtedly would be in his face the moment he hopped off the plane in Benin.

Osanobua! It was indeed a mess!

He stepped away from her and the door, giving her space and opportunity to make her exit. A part of him hoped she would leave even as another part of him silently begged her to stay. They stood staring at each other, neither of them moving or speaking, each waiting to see what the other would do. Soon it became clear that she was not going to leave.

"Maybe I should stay," she whispered, finally finding her voice. "I want to stay."

"I am a dangerous man, Mystery," he warned.

"That's okay," she answered. "I am a dangerous woman myself."

"You are a crazy woman," he clarified. "There is a difference."

She shrugged. "Whatever. I know what I want."

He shook his head as he stepped forward and covered the distance between them. She was making this hard for him. Why didn't she just leave and spare them both the heartache that was sure to come? She was clearly a woman who didn't think much about the consequences of her actions, and he was a man who had been raised to always consider the consequences of his dealings before acting, not after. The rebellious boy he had been, the boy who damned the consequences, was being stirred by this woman with her devil-may-care attitude to life. The longer she stayed, the harder it was for the sensible man he had become to quiet the unruly boy he had once been.

"No. You *think* you know what you want." As she opened her mouth to disagree, he put a finger over her lips and silenced her. "If I take your virginity tonight, you are mine. Mine *alone*. Mine *forever*. I will not only be your first, but I will be your last. Do you understand?"

He watched her reaction to his words. First, her eyes widened in shock and twinkled with anticipation. Evidently, she considered his proposition an exhilarating adventure.

Did she possess a bone of seriousness in that body of hers?

he wondered.

"Do you understand what I am saying and the implication of my words?" he demanded. He needed to make sure she appreciated the significance of his words. This was not a romance novel. This was the real world. If he touched her tonight, she was bound to him and his complex world.

She nodded as though she did not trust herself to speak.

"Is this still what you want?"

Again, she nodded, but he shook his head. "No. I need to hear you say it."

"Make me yours, Owen," she said eventually. "I want you to be the only man who ever touches me."

He lifted her chin so that he was staring intently into her eyes. He sensed all her emotions; the dread, of not knowing for sure what she was getting into. It was mixed with the thrill of secrecy and topped off with an unconcealed longing for him, a longing that equated his yearning for her.

"As you wish," he declared triumphantly as his mouth came down on hers, and he wrapped his arms tightly around her.

Eki opened her eyes just before dawn and stretched. Finally, she had done it. She was a woman. Every part of her felt sore, but she loved it. What a night it had been. It had turned out even better than she had anticipated, and she could not have chosen a better partner to share the experience with. It was hard to believe she had only just met him. She had repeatedly experienced a sense of déjà vu like she had been with him before, although that was not possible as she had never known any man that intimately before last night.

They had made love thrice. He had been gentle, passionate, and intense. He seemed to know her body so well, to know what gave her pleasure. She had never experienced anything like it. While she had dated Odaro, although they had never had sex, there had been a lot of kissing and cuddling, and not once did she feel the way she had done last night. His every touch had made her want him more. It was like her body was made for his and his for hers.

She had relished every moment of her time with him, but this was not a relationship she could pursue. She had a flight to catch. It was time to return and join Aiai and the others to leave for the airport. If she was late and Aiai had to reschedule their flights, she would be in a lot of trouble.

Eki got out of the bed gently, not wishing to rouse him. With any luck, she would be dressed and out of the hotel before he stirred. She turned to look at him. He was fast asleep. He looked exhausted but relaxed. Even in his sleep, he looked like a king. He was lying on his back one hand placed on his torso and the other thrown over his head. His chest was bare as the plain white sheets covered him only from the waist down. He had a beautiful body; strong arms, legs, and thighs that bore testimony to many days spent in the gym. It was a body to die for.

She recalled how that body had felt against hers and brought her pleasure again and again through the night, and her body ached with longing. A part of her wanted to crawl back into bed with him and lie in his arms. She remembered how safe she had felt as they had spooned together like a couple that had been married for years. She had been so content in his arms. It had felt like home, like she belonged there.

This is crazy! she screamed inside.

She had to get out of here before she got herself into trouble. She came out to lose her virginity, not her heart. Although she felt it was a little late for that. It seemed she had been losing her heart to this handsome stranger bit by bit throughout the night. She refused to dwell on that now. She crept around the room, gathering her things, and dressing quickly and quietly. She looked in the mirror before she exited the room. Her makeup was slightly smudged but remained intact, so she promptly touched it up and reapplied her lipstick. As she closed the door quietly behind her, she felt a pang of regret. She wished things had been different, and she had been able to know him. She realised though that she couldn't always have what she wanted.

When she arrived at Aiai's house, Aiai and the girls were awake, and she groaned. She had been hoping to sneak in and have a shower before facing anyone.

"Well, the fact that you're coming back this morning tells me that everything went according to your plan," Aiai stated by way of greeting as Eki entered the kitchen.

"Yep!" she answered drily. "Virginity's gone pop like a balloon."

"There goes our royal wedding."

"Yes. And I may well be pregnant too." That much was true. They had not used a condom the first time, and he had apologised for his thoughtlessness as he did have condoms with him in his luggage. The second and third time, she had prevented him as she did not see the need.

"Seriously, Eki?" Aiai asked in horror. "Is there no end to your foolishness?"

"It appears that there isn't," Amenze responded, walking into the kitchen. She turned to wink at Eki before pouring herself a cup of coffee. "I want to hear every juicy detail."

"You are no better than she is," Aiai chided. "You should be talking some sense into her head right now instead of asking for the juicy details."

Amenze shrugged. "Aiai, the way I see it, the damage has already been done. If she's pregnant, she's pregnant. No turning back the clock. She might as well spill her guts and tell us how she conceived the little bundle of joy we will be swapping care for any day now."

Aiai raised her hands and shook her head furiously. "Oh, no. Count me out of that arrangement. If she's pregnant, she will sort out childcare all by herself, I have a baby of my own to care for, and Efe wants another baby within the coming year, so my hands are full."

Amenze shrugged unperturbed, "Cousin T and I will take turns changing diapers. I love aunty duties. You get to dote on the little ones and hand them back to their parents as soon as they become a handful."

"You know, I wish you would both stop talking about me as if I am not here. If Owen and I have made a baby, I can take care of it all by myself, thank you very much." Eki paused to pout and added after a moment's reflection, "Plus I could always get a maid."

Amenze and Aiai exchanged looks. "Now that's the Eki we all know and love," Amenze said, and they both laughed.

"Thank God for maids," Aiai stuttered in between laughs.

"It's not funny," Eki said in mock anger.

"What's not funny?" Tiyan asked as she joined them in the kitchen.

"The short of it is that Eki has not only lost her virginity, but she may also be pregnant. There is the likelihood that in nine months, you will move from Cousin T to Aunty T," Amenze explained.

Tiyan stared at Eki with narrowed eyes. "Did you really do it?"

"Yes, I did." Eki smiled with a faraway look in her eyes.

"Was he Caucasian?"

"Is that all you can ask?" Amenze demanded. "Wouldn't you like to know what happens if she turns out pregnant and he denies paternity? What will Uncle Zogie and Aunty Ayi say?"

Tiyan rolled her eyes. "Just in case you've forgotten, the entire purpose of this exercise was to rile and shame Uncle Zogie and Aunty Ayi. So, the angrier they are, the better," she retorted and turned to Eki. "Answer the question. Was he White? Asian? Chinese? Arab?"

"No. He was African American," Eki replied.

"I thought you said you were going to pick any ethnicity for this deal apart from African. What happened to change your mind?" Amenze demanded.

Eki sighed wistfully. "He happened. Oh, you should have seen him stroll into that bar as though he owned it. And when he walked up to me and spoke, he had the deepest baritone I had ever heard mixed with a sexy American accent."

Aiai frowned, "Nothing sexy about an American accent," she muttered. Eki was in another world and failed to hear her.

"He was easily the tallest man in the room and had a runner's body, and you should have seen his chest, and arms and legs and thighs, oh my!" she sighed. "He was every woman's dream, *my* dream. He looked like he had stepped out of the front cover of GQ magazine. And those eyes, how he undressed me with them. And those lips, he was such a good kisser. He was such a gentle and generous lover, and oh when he…"

"Enough!" Aiai shouted, holding her palms over her ears. "I am a married woman, and there are certain things I should not hear." She turned to leave the kitchen. "We have a flight to catch ladies, let's prepare."

"We're not married; we want to hear every juicy detail," Amenze protested, and she and Tiyan pulled bar stools and sat on either side of Eki at the breakfast bar.

"Ladies!" Aiai screamed at them. "What part of we have a plane to catch did you not understand? Eki, save the scandalous chat for when we're at the airport, and I have my earbuds on."

Well, Aiai had spoken, and they all dispersed running upstairs to pack their bags, shower, and dress.

CHAPTER FIVE

She was gone. Osad knew it even before he turned and saw her side of the bed was empty. And she was not in the bathroom or the living room that adjourned the bedroom. She was gone, gone from his suite of rooms and his life.

Why? Had she not felt the same way? Had he been the only one who had sensed the chemistry between them? He groaned and buried his head in her pillow, inhaling the scent of her; the fragrance that had driven him wild last night. He had to find her. He was not ready to let her go.

First, he had a plane to catch. He had overslept due to his being awake most of the night and jet-lagged. His sisters were travelling with him and were already on their way to the airport. Sky King would not fly without him. He had to go, but once he had set in motion his coronation ceremony, he would look for her, his one-of-a-kind Mystery Lady.

She was *his*. And now she also had that which belonged to him. He had given her his seed. He knew that they had made a baby last night. He didn't need the chief priest of Benin Kingdom to tell him this, as crown prince and now Oba, there were some things that he knew for himself, and this was one of them. That child was a prince or a princess of the Benin Kingdom and would be raised accordingly.

What had he been thinking?

The truth was, he hadn't been thinking at all. He had never been careless with his seed. His father had warned him regarding that countless times. A responsible king did not father children indiscriminately. He had heed that advice; he had never given a woman his seed. Until now. And she had disappeared without a trace. But he would find her. She was his, the child was his, and he always returned for what was his.

"When did she leave?" he queried Sato, who entered his room as he finished dressing.

"I saw her leave about an hour ago. Would you

have wanted me to stop her?" he asked.

Osad was incognito and did not wish for his identity to be known. Sato had learned from years of working with Osad that he never wished Sato to make himself known as he never wanted people to tell that he moved around with a security detail. Hence, Sato always blended into the background and made himself as inconspicuous as possible.

Osad thought for a moment and shook his head. "No. It's fine. I did not want you to prevent her from leaving," he said. Then he paused and added, "I did not expect her to leave without giving me her contact details. I need you to find her. Not now. We have a plane to catch, and there are tons of things waiting for our attention in Benin, but once we settle in, I want you to return to London and find her. If need be, bring her to Benin."

"Is that wise, Osad? I mean there is the woman in Benin that you are expected to marry. Don't you think…" his voice trailed off as he realised his error.

"You are walking into a minefield, Sato. Watch

your step," Osad warned.

"Yes, my king." Sato bowed in obeisance.

When they arrived at the airport, Sky King was waiting for them on the tarmac. It was a glamorous sweetheart of a jet, painted white with a gold stripe that ran on either side from its front to rear. On its tail, it bore with pride the Ada and Eben royal symbols of the Benin Kingdom. The interior was a vision to behold; it boasted twenty oversized VIP reclinable seats covered in soft leather. With a finishing of smoked oak wood veneer, marble, and lush carpeting, it promised unique comfort and luxury that matched those of a five-star hotel suite. Flying Sky King was pure joy. Osad left Sato to sort out their bags as he jogged up the short flight of stairs.

"Finally! *Osaruese*! His Worship has arrived!" Ivie threw up her hands in mock relief as Osad entered the luxury lounge where all four of his sisters were seated enjoying pre-departure beverages.

She was his eldest sister and the only one who

could speak to him that way. To Ivie, he would always be her little brother. Besides, as the king's first child, she held a highly esteemed position in the family and the kingdom, and Osad had grown to accept and respect that. They were also great friends; much had been expected of both that had not been expected of their other siblings, and they had bonded over their shared responsibility.

"Cut him some slack. He flew in from America only last night. He must be exhausted, and his body must be struggling to catch up with the time zones," Orobosa stated, rising from her seat to hug him.

Orobosa, or Oro as he often called her, was his favoured sister and the family's baby. She was precious to her siblings; the entire family doted on her. Ivie was the first, and she was two years older than Ewere, the second born. There was also a two-year gap between Ewere and Osad and another two between Osad and Omo. When it seemed their parents had stopped having babies, Orobosa was born when Omo was five years old, and Osad was seven.

To date, he remembered his mother, Queen Esohe, placing in his arms the most adorable baby he had ever seen. She had become his treasure from that day, and he had fussed over her and indulged her, so she had become terribly spoilt. She was the only one of his sisters he had never refused anything. Well, he had never refused her anything until he came between her and his best friend, Edosa Aihie, with his buddy and sister, Ivie, playing the role of accomplice.

All was good now. Edosa and Orobosa were happily married and watching them last night, as Edosa held his wife when the news was broken, Osad knew he could not have asked for a better husband to take care of his baby sister.

"Thank you, Oro." He wrapped his arms around her and kissed the top of her head.

She smiled and looked up at him. "How are you holding up?" she asked. "I'm here if you want a cuddle or anything."

"*Emwanta*!" Omo mocked. "He is a man. He doesn't need a cuddle."

"That's where you're wrong. Even men need cuddles!" Orobosa stated and hugged Osad again.

Osad laughed. He needed a cuddle but not from his sister. Not that he would tell her that. The cuddle he craved right now was one that only his Mystery Lady could provide. But she was unavailable. He winced as he was reminded of waking up in an empty bed.

"Are you okay, Osad?" Orobosa asked. Doubtless, she had felt him recoil.

"I'm fine," he reassured her and hugged her back to the chagrin of his other sisters.

"Listen, Orobosa; this boy is going to be king in a couple of weeks. Don't turn him into one of the cuddly toys in your never-ending collection of stuffed animals," Ivie scolded.

"Ivie, did you just call him a boy?!" Omo gasped.

"You know, she is my father's mother, so she

does what she likes." Osad threw over his shoulder at Omo.

Their father had always called Ivie, *Iye*, thus referring to her as his mother, because she of all his children bore the most remarkable resemblance to her paternal grandmother.

"Osad, don't you dare go there!" Ivie warned. She hated to be reminded of her resemblance to her grandmother. It was not that she didn't love her grandmother, it was just that she thought she had not been a gorgeous woman and Ivie loved to think of herself as beautiful.

"Grandma!" Osad said, taking a step backwards as Ivie pretended to rise from her seat.

"*Osanobua!* I hate it when I have to do anything with my siblings," Ewere stated matter-of-factly looking up from the magazine she was reading. "Enough of the fooling around already and be seated for take-off. We are now running behind schedule. We must leave promptly."

"The plane doesn't go anywhere until I say so,"

Osad informed her.

Ewere was not the one calling the shots here. This was not one of the planes in the royal fleet that his sisters commandeered whenever they wanted. This was Sky King and only available to him and his father. With his father gone, he alone called the shots. His sisters were hitching a ride and Ewere ought to be reminded of that fact. She was one sister who repeatedly sought to take the reins of leadership from him, and he was not going to put up with her forwardness today. She may be older, but as she had often been told growing up, Osad was king.

"Did you hear that, Madam?" Ivie chided. "The plane doesn't leave until His Worship says so. If you are in a hurry, you will need to look for alternative means of transport."

Ewere held up a hand towards Ivie's face and buried her head once again in her magazine. "On the return flight, I assure you, I will."

"You are in my preferred seat, sis," Osad said to Ivie.

"And so, what? You want me to stand up for you, Your Worship?" she asked wide-eyed.

Osad sighed and rolled his eyes. She would never see reason. What was the point?

"Never mind. I see you are spoiling for a fight. Well, I will not give you one. You can have the seat as a good gesture from one sibling to another."

He moved further into the cabin and dropped into the seat beside Orobosa.

By the time they landed at the Benin airport, they had all changed from the western attires they had worn for the journey into traditional Benin attires worn by members of the Benin royal family. Two white Mercedes Benz limos were waiting for them. Each limo was followed by a land cruiser carrying armed plainclothes police officers. Fortunately, the press was not in sight. They were obviously at the palace awaiting the press conference arranged by the palace PR office.

The first limo would convey Osad and Sato to the Oba's palace where Osad would view his father's body and enter a meeting with palace chiefs culminating in a press conference. The second limo was for his sisters and would transport them to the queen mother's palace to lodge for their stay. Their husbands would join them there when they arrived, and there, they would receive any visitors who wished to see them.

Orobosa embraced him before they parted. "Be strong, Osad," she whispered.

"I will." He kept his voice steady as he kissed her head and looked at Ivie, who stepped forward and pulled Orobosa into her arms.

"Go on, Osad," she encouraged. "I'll take care of them."

Osad nodded. He knew she would. It had been like this since they were children, while he played the role of father, Ivie played the role of mother. He needed her now more than ever to look after their siblings as he faced the task that lay ahead of him not just tonight but in the coming days and weeks as he transitioned from crown prince to king.

The atmosphere in the Oba's palace was filled with tension that was so thick it could be cut through with a knife. Many palace chiefs were present and holed up in the throne room waiting for the crown prince. While some would doubtless be suspicious of the happenings, none would know for sure what secret was being kept from them until Osad addressed them. In another part of the north wing, in one of the large conference rooms, the members of the press were also waiting to be briefed by him.

Osad ignored both groups and journeyed with Usi Isekhure, to the king's residence in the south wing of the palace, to see his father. Tradition dictated that the Oba was embalmed and remained at home and not placed in the morgue. As they walked, following the plush palace passageways, all the servants bowed their heads, no one wanting to make eye contact with their new king.

Finally, they entered the king's residence and were received by his head servant, who led them to the king's chamber. Osad halted in his tracks as he saw his father, Oba Idahosa Edoni, lying in the massive bed amongst the finest Egyptian cotton sheets. Anyone would think he was fast asleep. He looked so peaceful and at rest.

Osad approached the bed even as he waved Usi and the servant out of the room. He wanted to be alone with his father one more time. He leaned over and touched his father's face. His skin felt different. Only then did the reality of the situation hit him.

"It is true. The great white chalk is indeed broken," he said to no one in particular.

He sank to his knees and bowed his head. His shoulders felt heavy with the weight of the kingdom that was currently his to bear. At that moment, he related with his father and what his life on the throne must have been like. Once again, he felt alone and empty. His father had always been there to guide him; without that guidance, he doubted he could embark on this journey. He lifted his head and looked at the man lying before him; the man he loved more than life itself. He would not fail him. His father had given him everything; the least he could do was make him proud. There was a tightness in his chest as he spoke.

"I'm sorry I wasn't here with you, Dad. I am sorry that you were alone, and I didn't share the burden with you as much as I should have. I am sorry I wasn't always the son I could have been, but I promise you that I will not fail you now. I will make you proud." He rose to his feet.

The meeting with the palace chiefs and the press conference passed quickly in a blur. Osad did not remember what he had said and what had been said to him; however, the news was out, and the kingdom had been thrown into mourning. He was exhausted and desired to retire to his bed in the palace of the Edaiken of Uselu. Still, he had one final meeting to attend with Chiefs Isekhure and Ezomo. It was impromptu, and he was annoyed when he realised that the topic on the agenda was his marriage.

As Usi spoke of Chief Alile's daughter, and how she was handpicked for him by the gods, Osad struggled to pay attention. His mind was on one woman alone, Mystery. He remembered their night; how well their bodies had fit, and how responsive she had been to his touch and he to hers. What would he not give at present to have her waiting for him in his bed when he left this futile meeting, which in his opinion was a waste of his time?

"What do you think, Your Highness?" Usi asked interrupting Osad's musing.

"What do I think about what?" he asked with a sigh.

Usi grinned. He knew Osad hated to hear anything concerning Chief Alile's daughter and that he had zoned out as he often did when her matter was mentioned.

"What do you think about Chief Alile bringing his daughter to meet with you at the Edaiken's palace tomorrow?" Usi repeated. "I am sure you will feel differently about marrying her once you have met her in person."

He raised his eyebrows. "Suppose I decide not to

marry Alile's daughter or a Benin woman?"

Usi gasped in shock. Clearly, the chief priest, who could see the future had not seen that one coming. Before he responded, Chief Ezomo hijacked the conversation.

"Your Highness, if you will permit me to speak," he began and waited for Osad's nod of approval before continuing. "The king makes the rules. As king, your father should have changed the rules to enable you to marry any woman you desire. He did not, but you can change that once you are king. However, you need a woman beside you when you are crowned.

My suggestion is that you pick a woman at this time and if dissatisfied with her, you can put her away and pick another once you are king. I appreciate your worries regarding Alile's daughter. She is not by any means a woman of your standing, and I see no reason why you should marry her because of some dream that the late Chief Amadin Isekhure had concerning her…."

"I will not sit here and have you insult my late father and his service to this kingdom." Usi cut him off abruptly. "May I remind you that this is the same woman your son was going to marry and that he is currently married to her older sister, the second daughter of Alile?"

"If my son is a fool and chooses to marry a woman below his social status, that is no reason for me to encourage His Highness to tow the same path," Chief Ezomo snarled.

Usi grunted but said nothing in response and Chief Ezomo turned his focus back to Osad.

"Your Highness, the Benin Kingdom is filled with a multitude of beautiful well-educated girls; girls whose parents have spent good money to educate them abroad. In the days following, and leading up to your coronation, families will be visiting you at your palace to commiserate with you, suppose every noble family in the land presents their unmarried daughter or daughters to you? Surely, from amongst the daughters of the wealthy in the land, you will find yourself a suitable woman. My daughter Ede has left Benin for the US, but I shall ask her to return right away, and I will be presenting her to you formally once she arrives."

Usi who had been staring at Chief Ezomo in disbelief, suddenly burst out laughing.

"Chief Ezomo, is there no end to your scheming to buy the throne of the kingdom of Benin? During the reign of Oba Edoni, you visited the Middle East where you impersonated him, leading your business associates to believe that you were the Oba of Benin. Moreover, you purported to offer chieftaincy titles to visiting business associates of yours from Asia. You also attempted to host your traditional festivals in defiance of Oba Edoni. Now, you seek to be the father-in-law of the next Oba of Benin. It will not happen. I will not allow you to put the throne of the Benin Kingdom in your pocket during my lifetime."

Chief Ezomo slammed his fist on the table. "Be careful how you speak to me, boy!"

Usi sneered, not the least bit perturbed by the

older man's anger. "I may be a boy, but I am the chief priest of the Benin Kingdom and head of the council of chiefs. In the latter position, I am your boss, and you will do well to remember that."

Chief Ezomo turned to Osad to intervene. Osad contemplated the older man's proposition for a moment and made his decision.

"I will see all the daughters from the noble families of the land starting tomorrow and then I will decide who to marry," he said to Chief Ezomo before turning to address Usi directly. "Alile is not a member of the noble class in this kingdom but to appease you and my father, I will allow him to present this famous daughter of his to me. I am sure you will be only too eager to convey the message."

He rose to his feet, bringing the meeting to an end. Chief Ezomo bowed and left the room, but Usi lingered.

"I beg you in the name of all that you hold precious not to marry Ezomo's daughter," he pleaded once they were alone. "Do not even consider it; it will be the beginning of the end of the kingdom."

"If you are certain Alile's daughter is the one for me, you have nothing to fear," Osad taunted.

"She is the one and, once you meet her, you will know it too," Usi asserted.

"I can't wait," Osad mocked and exited the room.

Sato was waiting for him in the grand Oba Eweka Hallway. Together they walked towards the north entrance where the limo was waiting to take Osad home.

"You will return to London tomorrow and find the woman from last night. Get another security personnel to stand in for you while you're away. You have seven days. If you don't find her, you don't return. Do you understand?"

"Yes, Your Highness," Sato responded, bowing his head.

CHAPTER SIX

"I don't believe it. Please tell me that it isn't true," Eki wailed, as she flung herself on her bed and wept softly into her pillow.

Only last night she had returned home after touring Dubai, Paris, and London with Aiai, Tiyan and Amenze. She had been excited and looking forward to what was to come next. She had also made a mental note to visit Oba Edoni and tell him about her trip and Owen. He would have been disappointed in her, but it was not as though his son had agreed to marry her, or proposed to her. The arrogant man had not even consented to meet with her in person. That was all in the past now. There would be no more visits to the palace for her in the future. She would not visit Oba Edoni or have the delight of spending time in his company. It was over, although she found it hard to believe. She had seen him the night before her trip. He had been so full of life. What had happened to him? She had only been gone for two weeks.

But he could not be gone. This had to be a rumour.

"I'm afraid it is true, Eki." Her father's words and grim look confirmed her fears. "The great white chalk is broken."

"I saw him before I left on my trip!" she lamented. "He didn't even say goodbye."

Her father sighed. "I know how you feel, Eki. The whole kingdom has been thrown into mourning since the news was announced last night, first to the palace chiefs and then the press via a press conference held by the Edaiken of Uselu," he stated.

The crown prince was in Benin? Of course, he was. He would be crowned king in his father's stead.

With his father out of the way, he would never marry her. He would choose any other woman provided she was Benin. Eki was pleased. She was finally rid of the horrid man. She placed a hand over her stomach and hoped she was pregnant with Owen's child. She knew where the future was taking her. She would return to London to search for Owen and beg him to forgive her and give them another chance. She did not know how she would find him, but she would try. He was a wealthy man; how hard would he be to find? If she only knew his last name. She should have left him her number. Or better still, waited for him to wake up or woken him up. How had he reacted when he woke up and found her gone and without any contact details? What had she done?

God, please help me to get him back, she prayed silently.

"Eki, there is something I need to tell you," her father announced, and the seriousness in his voice caused her to sit up and compose herself.

"What is it?" she asked, hugging her pillow to herself.

"Tomorrow, we will visit the crown prince at the Edaiken's palace where he is receiving guests in the days leading up to his coronation. We will go as a family to commiserate with him, and you will be formally presented to him."

Eki rolled her eyes. *Here we go again! The man did not want her. She had come to terms with the blatant truth. When would other people accept it?*

"How fabulous. I presume that during this meeting, we will magically fall in love as the prophecy says?" she asked sarcastically. She was already in love with another man. There was no room left in her heart now.

"Sarcasm doesn't become you, Ekinadoese. Behave," her father warned. "I want you to be on your best behaviour as we visit the crown prince at his palace. None of your shenanigans will be tolerated. I am a chief in this kingdom, and you will not bring me shame." He rose to his feet and left her room, shutting the door gently behind him.

Eki scoffed. "Father, you are about to be christened, Zogie "Shame" Alile. Wait until the whole kingdom hears how you tried to get your pregnant daughter to marry the future king of the Benin Kingdom."

She smiled and once again placed her hand over

her belly. She was Owen's and Owen's only. What if Crown Prince Osad Edoni had changed his mind and now wanted her? Would he marry her if another man had touched her, or worse, she was carrying another man's child? Her parents were about to be disgraced big time. Served them right! That would teach them to give her fiancé to her sister!

The next day Eki was fussed over by a group of women as they prepared her to visit the crown prince. Aiai, Tiyan and Amenze were making the trip to see the crown prince as well, Amenze opting to go with Eki's family instead of her parents. They were all dressed in the Benin traditional attires, and their hair had been wrapped in coral beads. They loved the traditional clothes, so they had only been too pleased to cooperate with the women that Ayi had hired to help them dress.

Eki, on the other hand, loathed dressing in the traditional attire because getting her hair up in the heavily beaded hairstyle was always an excruciating experience. As her hair was pulled in different directions and braided into the traditional style, she glared at her mother in the mirror.

"What is this fuss all about? Anyone would think that my bride price was to be paid today." She was exasperated and hoped her voice conveyed the displeasure that she so strongly felt.

"Please keep still and let the women do the job they've been contracted to do. You are a Benin woman going to visit her fiancé, who is a Benin king. How do you expect to dress, miss-know-it-all?" Ayi snapped, matching Eki's anger with some of her own.

What she had to be annoyed about baffled Eki. She was getting what she wanted, wasn't she? Or at least she thought she was. She did not know that Eki was about to pull an Eseosa on the family.

"Technically, he is not my fiancé, and he is not king until his coronation," Eki muttered under her breath.

It was late in the afternoon when they arrived at the palace of the Edaiken of Uselu. It was considerably smaller than the Royal Palace of the Oba of Benin but no less lavish. They were shown into a large State Room, which reminded Eki of some of the State Rooms in the Oba's palace. The opulence on display was breath-taking, from the massive crystal chandelier that hung low from the ceiling and descended several feet into the centre of the room, to the gold fabric sofa suite with trimmings that appeared to be gold plated. Never mind the array of mirrors and ancient Benin bronze artworks, which vied for attention with more modern sculptures crafted in delicate porcelain.

Refreshments were served, but Eki neither ate nor drank. She sat, with her head bowed, and her hands tightly clasped in her laps, refusing to make eye contact with Aiai, Amenze and Tiyan. This was a defining moment for her. If the prophecy was correct and they fell in love at first sight, then what?

She was no longer a virgin and was likely carrying another man's child, so it would be impossible for them to marry. She would be devastated if she fell for him and was unable to marry him. She did wonder though how she could fall in love with him after being with Owen. Could he be better looking, and a better dresser? While he was likely more affluent, especially once he combined his wealth with his father's, Owen had to be swimming in plenty of money so he could not be significantly wealthier than Owen.

As she mulled over the matter in her heart, there was a commotion, as palace guards opened a set of double doors, and from the corner of her eye, she saw three men enter the room in a single file. As she wondered which one was the crown prince, she noticed her parents were rising to their feet. She began to rise with her head bowed and the veil covering her face. Aiai, Tiyan and Amaze had also risen and were blocking her view.

The men parted, and the one in the middle came forward. Eki did not have a clear view to see him. Still, She could tell he was dressed in a traditional attire similar to the one worn by his companions; a white wrapper tied around the waist forming tidy pleats and falling to the ground with accurate precision. It was matched with a traditional white short-sleeved fitted shirt with the royal sceptres of the Ada and Eben embroidered on the face. Traditional coral beads on the wrists and neck completed the attire.

Her father addressed him, so she was confident he was the crown prince. She heard her father say that he had come with his family to commiserate with him. The man did not respond, and her father took her by the hand led her forward and pulled off her veil.

"Your Highness may I present to you my daughter, Eki. Ekinadoese. She is a lawyer by training." Chief Alile declared, his voice beaming with pride.

Osad froze as her veil came off, and he was face to face with the most beautiful woman he had ever laid eyes on. He had thought Mystery was captivating, but this woman gave a whole new meaning to the word. Or maybe it was that he appreciated her more because she was dressed in the Benin traditional attire. She had even reinvented the standard red wrapper that the Benin women tied over their chests, and in its place, she wore a red strapless three-tiered chiffon dress. It hugged her beautiful lean figure, and he would be content to look at her all day. One thing was sure; he could never argue with the fact that she would make an ideal arm candy if he was looking for arm candy.

Eki briefly forgot that royal protocol prevented her from looking at the king's face. As her veil came off, she lifted her head, and her eyes met his disapproving ones. In that instant, she realised that he was….

"Ah! Oh, God!" she gasped, and her hands came up to cover her mouth and stifle a scream, albeit too late. She stepped backwards, wanting to get as far away from him as possible but bumped into Aiai who restrained and steadied her. Anyone would have thought she had seen a ghost. She was visibly shaken, but quickly appreciated that this must be unacceptable behaviour in the presence of her future king and attempted to remedy the situation.

"I – I – I – er – I – Your Maj – er – high –" she sighed. It was no use; her brain wasn't cooperating with her mouth. She may as well be silent. She looked up at him once again, this time raising only her eyelids.

Hmmm. Osanobua! What a clumsy and ridiculous woman! Osad mocked. He carried on his internal dialogue all the time, fixing her with a hard stare.

But God, she was beautiful. If only she had half a brain.

And to think I was worried she wouldn't be able to string together words in English. She can't even string together syllables!

Awkward. Blundering. Inept. Irresponsible. Disorderly. He ruminated. *How did she become a lawyer?*

Proud. Prejudiced. Arrogant. Overbearing. Highhanded. She mused as she recalled his condescending words to his father regarding her two years ago. *Who did he think he was?* Anger stirred inside her. She raised her eyelids to look at him again.

Osad felt his body stir as she looked at him from beneath her lashes. Promptly, he reproved himself.

Do not lust after her beauty. Do not let her take you with her eyelids.

He had to get out of here quickly. He did not like what she was doing to him with those eyes of hers.

Jezebel. A destroyer of kings.

Chief Alile stared at Eki in bewilderment. "Ekinadoese! *Vba yo na kha?* What is the meaning of this?" he scolded. "Will you behave yourself?!"

"I think she is behaving herself, Chief Alile," Osad answered slightly irritated although he was more annoyed with himself than anyone else. He turned his attention to Usi, who was standing to his left-hand side, and who coincidentally was lost in his own little world. He followed his gaze to a young woman standing next to Eki. He sucked in his breath, impatiently. The fool could at least pay some notice to the disaster this meeting with Alile's daughter was fast becoming.

Osad was angry that he had allowed himself to be talked into finally meeting with Alile's daughter. Although truth be told, she was more beautiful than any of the women he had been introduced to thus far. But she was also apparently a nutcase judging by how she had just behaved which he was sure was typical.

"You failed to enlighten me as to her mental state," he growled, causing Usi to tear his eyes away slowly and reluctantly from Tiyan. He heard Eki gasp but completely ignored her. He would speak concerning her any way he wished; he was king, after all. Well, almost.

"Your Highness," Usi cleared his throat and thought of what to say to appease Osad; meanwhile his eyes darted to Tiyan once more, and Osad waved a hand dismissively and spoke to chief Alile and his family.

"While this has been very enlightening and

entertaining, I must take my leave. I have other commitments."

How rude. Utterly pompous. Entirely unqualified to be king. Eki thought. The man was as vile, as she had feared. But how had he been so different two nights ago? No. She would not think about that. She refused to think about being with him in London two nights ago. She would not consider her error and the consequences. Not here, not now, or she would scream and pull her hair out like the insane person he believed she was.

As Osad turned to leave the room, he said to Isekhure under his breath, "If I needed entertainment, I would have summoned the court jester."

"If His Highness would allow us a word," Chief Alile interrupted.

Osad looked at his best friend and brother-in-law who had flown in from London only that morning and was standing next to him, his brow raised. He had great respect and admiration for Edosa and occasionally looked to him for approval. Edosa understood the look, and he nodded quietly.

"Please be seated, everyone," he said as he sank into his ceremonial chair which had been a gift from his father when he was crowned Edaiken of Uselu and crown prince of the Benin Kingdom. It was designed after the similitude of his father's throne at the Oba's palace. His guests were seated before him, and Usi and Edosa flanked him. "Talk to me, Chief Alile."

"Thank you, Your Highness. I wish to apologise for my daughter's behaviour. I have no idea what came over her."

Osad observed Chief Alile in silence even as he recounted the events in his head. What had come over Eki Alile was the least of his troubles; he was more concerned about what had come over *him*. For more than two years, he had avoided meeting her and had made it clear that he wanted nothing to do with her, swearing her beauty wouldn't sway him. Yet when she appeared, the first thing he thought of was how beautiful she was. He must be mad.

"If my lord, the crown prince, will permit to speak," Mrs Alile began and continued to speak even though her lord, the crown prince, had not permitted her to do so. She was also oblivious to the fact that she was disrupting his reflections. "I must say that I have my reservations regarding this marriage. I know that your father desired you to marry Eki, but you see Eki is my daughter, and I know her better than anyone else, she is not ready for marriage. I must warn you that she is not able to cook or clean or carry out wifely duties…" Her voice trailed off as she realised that she had not been permitted to speak and that the crown prince wore an irritated look.

As he opened his mouth to address Mrs Alile, he caught a glimpse of Eki rolling her eyes, and he suppressed a chuckle before berating himself.

"If Eki could speak, these things that you mention would not be a problem."

For the second time that evening, he heard her gasp. His eyes sought her, and he observed that she was staring daggers at him. People generally avoided looking him in the eye. The women that had been presented to him so far had been demure in his presence. They kept their heads bowed, and eyes to the ground, but not this woman. At every opportunity, she looked him in the eye. She did have a spine it seemed. He would love to discover how resilient it was.

He rose to his feet. "Clear the room," he demanded addressing the palace guards who were standing at the various exit points. "I wish to be alone with Miss Alile." The guards opened the door and began to usher the guests out of the room.

"Usi and I will be in your office if you need us," Edosa informed him before turning to Usi. "Usi, let's go." His voice brooked no argument.

Osad hid a smile as Edosa issued an order to the chief priest of the kingdom. It was just like Edosa to dispense with protocol and carry on as though they were in private. Usi appeared not to mind and seemed only too pleased to flee Osad's presence seeing as the initial meeting with Osad and Eki had been a disaster contrary to his prophecy.

Once the room was empty, Osad walked slowly and deliberately towards Eki, arms behind him, eyes predatory. Her head was bowed, and her hands shook slightly.

Good, he thought. She would do well to be afraid.

He circled her, like a lion circling its prey. He intended to intimidate her, but once he was behind her, he could scarcely stop himself from checking her out.

Bloody hell! She was gorgeous.

"Do you like what you see, Your Highness?" she asked, shocking him out of his musing.

He frowned. *Had he heard her right?* He walked around her until he was facing her.

"What did you say?" he demanded.

She raised her head and looked at him. He saw the glint in her eyes. He was instantly reminded of his mischievous Mystery Lady. His heart ached, as he wondered where she was and what kind of crazy stunt she was up to. He had heard no word from Sato, but he knew he would find her. If anyone could find her, it was Sato.

"What surprises you more? The fact that I can speak at all, or the fact that I, a local Benin girl, can string together enough words to form a coherent sentence in English?" she asked, her chin lifted in defiance, albeit her eyes continued to sparkle.

"I find your boldness shocking, Miss Alile, and believe me when I tell you that there are very few things that surprise a man in my position." He lifted her chin, and they glared at each other, both refusing to back down.

"You expect me to be afraid of you?" she taunted.

"I am a dangerous man, Miss Alile. You would be a fool not to be," he glowered at her. "Crushing you would be as easy for me as doing this."

To demonstrate the ease with which he could devastate her, he approached the gold metal and glass side table on which was displayed the busts of a Benin king and queen crafted in delicate porcelain. The pair had been a gift from one of his western business associates, and he never liked it. A statue of a Benin king and queen was best cast in bronze. He knocked down the bust of the queen while holding Eki's gaze. The piece of pottery fell to the marble floor and shattered to pieces. From the corner of his eye, he saw a guard shift restlessly. His servants were usually uneasy when he "dropped" things. Over the years he had learned that doing so aroused fear in most people.

Eki, however, was not most people, as he was starting to learn. She did not flinch. She held his gaze even as her expression moved from perplexed to impish. Before he had a chance to speak, she walked up to him and mirroring his gesture, knocked down the bust of the king. It fell and shattered to pieces.

"I can crush you like that," she said then looked up at him and grinned wickedly for good measure.

Osad could not help himself as he grinned in response. She was baiting him, daring him to act on his threat. This was not a scared rabbit before him. This was a lioness. His mate. His equal.

Where had that thought come from? What was the matter with him?

This woman was not his mate. *Mystery* was his mate, and she was carrying his seed. Eki Alile though was tough; he would give her that. If any woman could survive being put away, once he became king and changed the rules to allow him to marry Mystery, it was the woman standing before him. And the fact that her father was poor meant his silence on the matter could be bought. Osad made up his mind in that instance. This was the woman he wanted. She was strong and able to withstand whatever he threw at her, including divorce, without breaking. Besides, she was unruly and needed taking in hand, and he was the man for the job.

CHAPTER SEVEN

"Oh!" Eki groaned. "That was a disaster. I am a complete disaster." She fell on the bed, glad it was finally over, and she was back home in the privacy of her bedroom.

"You can say that again," Amenze stated matter-of-factly.

"Oh. Not now, Amenze. I want to crawl into a hole, curl up and die or better still look for a bridge to jump off." She lay on the bed and covered her face with a pillow.

"What was that all about, Eki?" Aiai demanded as she barged into the room with Tiyan on her tail, who looked like she, too, had a million things to say.

Eki gave her a warning look and sat up to address Aiai. "You are not going to believe what I am about to say."

"Try me," Aiai goaded. "With your track record, anything is likely."

Eki groaned and fell back on the bed once more covering her head with a pillow. "That was Owen."

"Who was Owen?"

Eki sat up, throwing the pillow from her. "Crown Prince Osad Edoni is Owen."

Tiyan and Amenze gasped, in shock. Aiai shook her head in denial.

"No. You went to The Dorchester in London and met a man named Owen, and you had sex with him, you are possibly pregnant, end of the story." Aiai went over the details of Eki's escapade swiftly.

"No, Aiai. I thought it was the end of the story, but today when we visited the crown prince, I instantly identified him as Owen. Apparently, what happens in London doesn't stay in London," she winced.

"Yeah. It follows you to Benin," Amenze interjected sarcastically.

Aiai raised her hands to silence everybody. "Wait there a minute. Are you telling me that you slept with a man whose name you don't know?" she shouted. "Ekinadoese! *Ashawo*! *Igbi Agia*!" She took a step towards Eki, Eki shrank back, and Tiyan moved in between them.

"Calm down, Aiai. I understand how this might have happened. When Prince Osad Edoni travels around the world, he usually does so incognito unless on official duty. This means he uses an alias. His usual alias is Owen Morgan. Owen is one of his middle names; Morgan comes from his mother's maiden name, Aifuwa-Morgan. When he met Eki in London, he was obviously was using the alias Owen Morgan."

Yes. That was the Tiyan they all knew and loved. She knew a little bit about every topic under the sun. While the piece of information would have been useful a few days ago, now, it was useless, Eki thought dryly.

"You are telling me that Eki, in a bid to embarrass her parents and escape marriage to the crown prince, slept with Owen Morgan who is really Prince Osad Edoni." Aiai sought clarification.

"Yes. From where I'm standing, that's how it looks," Tiyan confirmed.

"Wow! What are the odds of that happening?" Amenze asked no one in particular.

"I don't get it. How could you not have known it was him?" Aiai queried. "All the time you visited Oba Edoni didn't you see a picture of his son anywhere?"

"No. All the family pictures are in the queen's residence, and I never stepped foot into the building. Also, Oba Edoni and I did not discuss his family much and apart from the times he wanted Osad and me to meet, we rarely discussed him. And I was never interested enough to Google him," Eki clarified.

"Hmm. I can see how you would not have known. If you were like Cousin T, who makes it her business to know a little bit of every matter under heaven, you would have spotted him a mile away and run for your dear life. Too late now. You've run straight into his arms." Amenze's voice held a hint of humour.

"You and your rotten luck!" Aiai yelled at Eki. She was not amused.

"Yeah," Amenze concurred. "Why didn't you choose a man from a different ethnicity as we all agreed? If handsome was what you wanted, I would have asked Dimitris to introduce you to a Greek god."

"She didn't want a Greek god; she wanted a Benin god." Tiyan jibed.

"You don't understand. When he walked into that bar that night, he was so handsome I couldn't resist him," Eki whined.

"She is right. He is good looking," Amenze agreed.

"Not as handsome as Usi Isekhure," Tiyan remarked dreamily.

"Hey, you," Aiai fixed her with a hard stare, "Do not get up to any foolishness. We have a serious matter to deal with, and the last thing we need is for you to further complicate it by losing your virginity to the kingdom's chief priest!"

"Don't worry about me. I won't be losing my virginity to Usi until after we are married," she said distractedly. "Did you know that at 28 years old Usi Isekhure is a virgin? His role as a chief priest means that he does not get to sleep with a woman until she is his wife. We are perfect for each other. He'll be taking my virginity while I'll be taking his."

"I don't even want to know how you happen to know that he is a virgin," Aiai said to Tiyan and glared at Eki. "What now?"

"Now, she has to marry him. Period!" Amenze said before Eki could speak.

"If he will have her; he didn't want her before, remember?" Aiai pointed out.

"True," Amenze replied. "But he would not have asked to be alone with her today if he was not contemplating marriage. Also, he didn't exactly reject her when they met in London. A man like that doesn't attempt to impregnate a woman he is just meeting unless he intends to keep her around for a long time."

"It was Mystery he met in London," Tiyan reminded them all. As though they had forgotten. As though they could forget.

"That is correct," Amenze acknowledged. "But Eki is Mystery. If he wanted Mystery, he wants Eki."

"You have a point," Aiai admitted.

"What point?" Eki objected, feeling the need to speak up. *How could they carry on as though she were not here?* "Amenze, what do you mean I have to marry him? What kind of solution is that?"

"You should have considered that before you gave yourself to him," Amenze retorted. "Do you remember that you pledged to be his? You vowed that he would be your first and last."

"I remember," Eki answered sombrely.

How had she been so daft? How had she not made the connection, the fact that he walked like a king and reminded her of Oba Edoni? This was chaos; she had outdone herself this time. All she had wanted was to embarrass her parents, and she had only ended up embarrassing herself and tied herself to a man she did not wish to marry.

If she had only known who he was that night, she would have run as fast as she could in the opposite direction. It was too late for regrets, the deed had been done, and she may be carrying the next Oba of Benin in her womb. As if she was not beating herself up enough, Amenze-the-realist continued laying down the consequence of her actions, in no unclear terms and forcing her out of her trance.

"Well, you may have done it in the heat of the moment, and you may have thought it was exceptionally romantic, like a loaded page in one of those silly romance novels that you read. This is the real world, however, and you are a Benin woman. I don't have to tell you the implication of what you have done. Osad Edoni is the new Oba of Benin. As Oba, he is one of the gods of this kingdom."

They all became quiet as the understanding of

Amenze's words hit home. Eki sighed. This was getting worse by the minute. *What had she done?*

"Yes. I remember the fable. There are four hundred and one deities in the Benin Kingdom, and the Oba of Benin is deity number four hundred and one. Hence he is called the monarch of the sky reigning on land." She did her best impression of her father's voice. How could she forget the myth that surrounded the Benin throne? If her father had told her the story once he had told her a million times.

"I am glad you remember. Gee, Uncle Zogie will be delighted." Tiyan jeered, and Eki shot daggers at her. Amenze ignored Tiyan's jibe and carried on with her tale of woes.

"He was your king, a god of this land when he bedded you. He asked you if you were his and you said yes. You may have run away from him the morning after but Eki, you are his, and sooner or later circumstances beyond your control will make it so. As the good book of the Lord says, with your mouth, you shall be justified or condemned."

The silence in the room intensified, if that was at all possible, as they all allowed Amenze's words to sink in.

"Amenze does have a point," Tiyan broke the silence. "But there is the virginity test which you will never pass now. So, there is a chance you can escape marrying the prince."

"And then what?" Aiai asked, looking at Eki. "The king; deity number four hundred and one has touched you; no Benin man will touch you with a barge pole unless he has a death wish."

"Yes, there is that Benin proverb that says, the tree the leopard has climbed the hyena cannot climb," Tiyan affirmed.

"Then I will leave the country. I will go back to the UK, pursue a doctorate, and marry a non-Benin man who doesn't care if I gave my virginity to the Oba of Benin."

"And if you are carrying the royal heir?" Amenze queried.

"I had not thought about that," Eki replied, sighing heavily.

"It seems to me that as usual, you had not thought about anything. This was all knee jerk reaction as it always is with you, Eki. I have covered your mess for years but no more. This time, you are going to put on some big girl pants and sort out yourself," Aiai said firmly.

Eki looked from her sister to her favourite cousin Tiyan and best friend Amenze, and from their facial expressions, it was clear they were not going to intervene and clean up her mess this time. For the first time in her life, she felt she was truly alone. She slumped on the bed.

"Oh! I'm definitely jumping off a bridge before the day is over," she declared tearfully.

At that instance, the door was flung open, and Ayi breezed into the room. She was all smiles and doubtless in a celebratory mood.

"I have some exciting news," she told Eki. "Chief Isekhure called your father. The crown prince has decided to marry you. He has delegated some members of the royal family to visit tomorrow and make all the necessary arrangements. You are going to be the queen. Now, I believe the prophecy of late Chief Amadin Isekhure."

"How quickly you change sides, Mother. You didn't seem to believe the prophecy when you were exposing Eki's faults to the crown prince only a few hours ago."

"Aisosa, what would you have me do? You know how problematic Eki can be. I wanted to protect myself. Is it a small thing to be the king's mother-in-law? I had to make my fears known as soon as possible so that if Eki's shortcomings come to light, he would not say he was not warned. Now that he knows, and has decided to marry her, we are safe from his wrath." She moved to sit on the bed beside Eki. "Nonetheless, if I offended you, my queen, my Oloi, I am sorry. Forgive your mother." She drew Eki into her arms and embraced her.

Eki smiled faintly. She wished she could be

genuinely happy, but all she could think was, *How on earth did I end up here, in the same place I was seeking to get away from?*

"It's fine Mother; I forgive you," she said in a voice she did not recognise. Thankfully, Ayi was lost in her world of joy, and she did not notice. As she waltzed out of the room, she stopped and spun around.

"Lest I forget, a car will be coming for you tomorrow morning to take you to the palace for your virginity test." With a smile, she walked out and shut the door behind her.

It was custom that before the king or the crown prince married a woman, she underwent a test to verify that she was still a virgin.

Eki sighed. *If you only knew what has become of my virginity, Mother, you would be wailing instead of celebrating.*

Amenze broke the silence. "I told you that you are his, and sooner or later circumstances beyond your control will make it so," she reminded Eki.

"Yeah. And I told you I was going to jump off a bridge," Eki sneered.

"If you fail the virginity test, which you will, you could always come clean and tell him you are Mystery," Tiyan offered.

Eki grunted and shook her head. "I'd rather jump off a bridge."

The following morning a car arrived to take Eki to the palace hospital for her virginity test. Eki travelled alone. Aiai and the girls had declined to accompany her. True to their word, they were leaving her to clean up her mess all by herself.

Or were they?

Tiyan had gone out the night before and hadn't come back home. Eki suspected she had gone out with Usi Isekhure. They had been giving each other strange looks at the Edaiken's palace the day before, and when the crown prince had asked that the guests leave the room, Eki was made to understand that Usi had seized the opportunity to have a quick private chat with Tiyan.

Later that night, Tiyan had dressed up and gone out, refusing to tell Eki who her mysterious date was, but Eki had looked out of her bedroom window and seen a blue Range Rover Sport pull up outside the front gate. A man who resembled Usi Isekhure had stepped out of the vehicle to help Tiyan get into the front passenger's seat. He was casually dressed in jeans and a polo shirt. Eki had only ever seen Chief Isekhure in traditional Benin attire, but she was confident the man from last night had been Usi. She had text Tiyan to confirm and received a smiley face by way of response. She exhaled. It seemed like her favourite cousin was determined to have the chief priest's virginity.

When she arrived at the hospital, situated in the north wing of the palace, Eki met with the assigned doctor who introduced herself as Dr Idah. She explained the procedure to Eki and showed her to a room where a nurse helped her prepare. As the doctor was a long time returning, the nurse left to fetch her. Only when she returned, the doctor continued to be missing, and she instructed Eki to get dressed.

"What's going on?" Eki asked a little puzzled.

"The doctor will explain. She is in her office," the nurse replied.

She never made it to the doctor's office because two men, who she guessed were palace chiefs, judging by their attire, intercepted her in the hallway. She recognised Chief Isekhure immediately, the other man she had seen the day before. He had been with the crown prince and Chief Isekhure when she had made a classic fool of herself.

"Eki," Usi said by way of greeting. "This is my friend, Chief Edosa Aihie."

"Hello." Eki wore a smile for both men.

"I have taken the liberty of cancelling the er-physical examinations," he said without much ado. "I have reason to believe that it is unnecessary."

Eki looked from Edosa Aihie to Usi Isekhure wondering what was going on and whether either man would tell her. Cancel the examinations? She had been brought here specifically for this reason. She had been told from the onset that it would happen before she married the crown prince. Why cancel it? Was the crown prince aware? What happened on their wedding night when he found her not to be a virgin?

"But I er –"

She paused as Chief Isekhure looked at her with eyes that bore into her, giving her the jitters. She felt like he could see into her soul; like he could see her offering up her virginity to the crown prince in his suite at The Dorchester. For the first time, she understood why he was a much-dreaded chief priest despite being so young.

"I see what others fail to see, Eki," he explained, his eyes never leaving hers. "Go home."

"Er – er – okay," Eki answered, her voice barely above a whisper, her heart thudding fast in her chest.

He smiled. "Relax," he assured her. "We're good."

He left her standing there. Edosa Aihie followed behind, stopping only to give Eki a reassuring smile. It was a smile that said, *I am in your corner*, which she thought was weird since she did not know him.

Why had Chief Isekhure cancelled the examination? Did he have information that she didn't? Had Tiyan said anything?

If she has revealed Mystery, I am going to kill her! Eki seethed.

Tiyan was home when she arrived, and so was Amenze. They excitedly informed of the visit of the royal family representatives.

"It's happening, Eki, and you are the envy of every young woman in Benin." Tiyan hugged her even before she had her foot in the door. "You are going to be the queen, the Oloi, according to prophecy."

"Oh yeah?" Eki asked wryly. "I suppose with a little help from you?"

Tiyan frowned. "What do you mean?"

"You were out with Usi all night, weren't you?"

"Wow! Tiyan!" Amenze giggled in exhilaration. "You never said a word. *Ashawo*."

"Oh, please. Just because I spent the night at his place doesn't mean we slept together. It's a big house, you know. It boasts ten bedrooms and twelve bathrooms."

"And you slept there. Why? Because you are homeless? I maintain that you are an *ashawo*."

"My virginity is still intact," Tiyan protested.

"What about his?" Amenze queried. "Is it still intact? Not that we will ever know. Is there a way to test a man's virginity?"

Eki burst out laughing despite herself. "Will you both stop this madness? You are making me lose my train of thought." She scowled at Tiyan. "Did you at any time last night, mention my one-night stand with Owen?"

"No. Why on earth would I do that?"

"I don't know why you would do it and if you

remember, yesterday when you asked me to come clean, I told you I'd rather jump off a bridge." She looked at Amenze. "I am not sure what's going on, but today when I arrived at the palace hospital for my test, Chief Isekhure cancelled it, just like that." She snapped her fingers. "I suspect Tiyan told him of my night with Owen."

"Yep," Amenze confirmed. "It must have come up during pillow talk."

Tiyan rolled her eyes. "I did not discuss you with Usi," she reiterated. "Usi is the chief priest; he is tuned into matters that concern the kingdom, especially the royal family. If he knows you are the one for the crown prince, he must also know that you are all right to marry him without needing a virginity test."

"Well, I can't argue with that. It makes perfect sense to me," Amenze said. "Anyway, Eki, this bolsters the point I made yesterday. You promised yourself to the man; you are his and events out of your control will make it so."

And so, they did. The next two weeks passed in a blur of activities as the palace and the entire kingdom prepared for the new Oba's coronation. Eki and her family were also extremely busy preparing for her wedding and subsequent move to the palace. She would marry Osad on the eve of his coronation after which she would be taken to the Edaiken's palace. They would officially move into the Oba's palace during the coronation ceremony the following day.

Over the fortnight, she saw nothing of Osad, but he ensured that she had everything required to transition to wife and queen. A personal shopper travelled to Paris and Milan to get a new wardrobe for her. Local dressmakers were commissioned to make uncountable traditional attires in keeping with her new status as queen and Oloi. No stone was left unturned, and the personal shopper did an excellent job; she had to admit that she could not have done a better job if she had made the trip herself.

She had the pleasure of meeting with Oba Edoni's daughters and their families. She liked them all, especially Orobosa, who was as carefree as she was, and Ivie reminded her of her dear sister, Aiai. If they knew anything of the tension between her and their brother, they did not let on. They appeared pleased with the woman he had chosen for a wife and were happy to welcome her into the family.

She was also introduced to the women who would be serving her in her new position of queen, her chief of staff, personal assistant, and head maid. She was granted access to the queen's residence at the Oba's palace to oversee and make her input into the refurbishments and redecorating. She dragged Aiai along as she was not only an architect but an excellent interior decorator and designed the interiors of all the houses built by Homes for Less. Together, they worked on making the queen's residence Eki's dream home. The house had belonged to Osad's mother, Queen Esohe, before her death and her things that had been locked up in the building were moved to the Queen Mother's palace where she would have lived following Osad's coronation had she been alive.

Osad's sisters and their families currently occupied the stately home as they awaited the coronation. It would be a week-long ceremony with a variety of traditional festivals. Three main events would be at the coronation week's forefront; the old Oba would rest with his ancestors. It would be a closed-door ceremony attended only by immediate members of the family and high-level chiefs. The new Oba would marry according to the Benin native law and customs, and the culminating ritual would be his formal ascension on the throne of his ancestors with his wife at his side. The Benin people would see their Oloi publicly for the first time.

CHAPTER EIGHT

Finally, the day came when Eki and Osad were to be wed. Eki stayed in bed until late in the morning; her mother insisted that she be pampered. She would never argue with pampering; she was all for it. The house was abuzz with activities when she got out of bed. The women hired to dress her helped her take a long luxurious bath. Afterwards, she had a light meal and sat before the mirror wearing a cream silk dressing gown. The next hour or so, she endured the torture as her hair was yanked, combed, plaited, and beaded as the women attempted to create a traditional okuku hairstyle befitting an Oloi.

Outside the house, and in the street, she could hear the commotion. Well-wishers lined the roads, leading to her father's house and some strived to forcibly enter the premises hoping to catch a glimpse of their new queen. But as was to be expected, the security was tight with palace guards, police officers and the crown prince's network of bodyguards all present to protect guests and forestall mischief-makers.

Key members of the royal family that had been delegated to attend the wedding at the bride's home were also arriving in large numbers in their flamboyant traditional clothes and luxurious cars that set them apart from commoners. The wedding would hold in two locations. The first location was the bride's home where a senior member of the royal family, in this case, the younger brother of Oba Edoni, His Royal Highness Prince Nosakhare Ezoti, would perform the necessary rites on behalf of the crown prince. After this, Prince Ezoti and the bridal party would escort the bride from her father's home to the palace of the Edaiken, where she would be formally handed over to her new husband.

The Edaiken's palace was location number two for the wedding ceremony. Other royal family members and high-level chiefs would be waiting with the crown prince to receive his wife amidst festivities. The royal couple would receive a blessing and retire to their chambers for the night while the partying amongst their guests continued all night.

Eki's hair was finally fixed, and her makeup done, and the women helped her into her dress. Today, like when she had visited the crown prince at his palace, Eki had discarded the traditional Benin wrapper and replaced it with a red strapless mermaid gown with a tiered ruffle skirt. Like the first gown, it hugged her slim figure, accentuating her curves. It was four-tiered, the top was made from a red hand-beaded and embroidered silk organza fabric, and the four-tiered skirt which began a little above her knees was made from the most delicate ostrich feather lace fabric.

It was a dream of a dress and made even more magnificent by the rare and expensive coral beads belonging to Queen Esohe, which were loaned to Eki by the Oba's palace. A pair of crystal-embellished satin pumps significantly boosted her height and added elegance to the attire.

"You look absolutely stunning, Your Highness!" Aiai exclaimed as she entered the room where Eki presently stood fully dressed, staring at herself in the full-length mirror.

Eki beamed. "Thank you, but none of that your highness nonsense from you," she warned.

Aiai laughed. "Yes, ma'am," she responded. "Dad wants you to come downstairs. The bride price has been paid, and it is time to hand you over to Price Ezoti formally."

As she spoke, she opened the door to reveal Amenze, Tiyan and, to Eki's delight, little Zena. They were her bridal train and wearing dresses like hers. They were waiting to escort her downstairs to the living room where she would be handed over to Prince Ezoti. Little Zena was beside herself with excitement.

"Look at my dress, Aunty Eki. It's exactly like yours," she announced and ventured to twirl around but was swiftly prevented by her mother, who reached out a hand to steady her.

Eki hid a smile. Poor Aiai. She had gone from mothering disorderly Eki to mothering little Zena who was proving to be as rowdy as her Aunty Eki.

"I need you to keep still for mummy, baby. We don't want you ruining your lovely dress," Aiai warned.

"Yes, mummy." Zena looked crestfallen.

"Don't worry, Zee. You can twirl for me later and show me your marvellous dress, although from what I can see, you look stunning like a princess."

Zena beamed. "Just like you, Aunty Eki."

She was so adorable at that moment that Tiyan and Amenze let out an, "Aww," and Eki blew her precious little niece a kiss.

"Okay. We need to go. We shouldn't keep Dad waiting," Aiai said. She looked at the women who had dressed Eki. "Please put her veil on," she instructed.

A red beaded organza veil was produced and thrown over Eki's head and shoulders. She walked past Aiai and fell into step behind Tiyan and Amenze. She reached out and took Zena's hand.

"Come on, Zee," she said. "Walk with Aunty Eki."

With Tiyan and Amenze going ahead and Aiai following behind, they made their way down the stairs and into the living room. Chief Zogie Alile received his daughter, and lifted Eki's veil slightly, enough for Prince Ezoti to identify her and be sure he was taking the right bride to his nephew. Next, he officially handed Eki over to the older man by placing her in his lap seven times. On the count of seven, the older man embraced her signalling her acceptance into the Benin royal family as the next king's wife.

Osad was in the dressing room adjoining his chambers being dressed in the traditional attire worn by Benin men during their marriage by native law and customs. Three senior members of the omuadas were tasked with the duty of helping him get dressed.

The omuadas were male servants who attended to the personal day to day needs of the Oba. They looked after the king and provided him with a wide range of services, from cleaning his chambers to serving his meals, from choosing his attires to bearing the royal sceptres. The most senior was also the king's head servant and authorised to enter the king's bedroom even while he slept. As he dressed, he was duly informed that the ceremony at the bride's family home was finalised, and she was on her way to him.

Bride. She was now his bride.

He found it hard to believe he was going through with this. Eki was a beautiful girl, and sleeping with her would be no hardship. His body yearned for it, and he had thought of little else since their disastrous meeting two weeks ago. Even the objections he'd initially had were not so strong after meeting her in person and learning from Usi Isekhure that she had just returned from a two-year trip in the UK where she had bagged two master's degrees with first-class honours.

He wasn't sure why she was somewhat awkward, and from all indications, even her mother had zero confidence in her. He would have been willing to teach her to help her grow if he did not resent so much the fact that he had not chosen her for himself and the woman that he had met by chance and selected for himself was at large. He was closing in on her though. Sato had returned from London only this week and reported that after some investigations he discovered that Mystery had taken a cab from The Dorchester to an address in Chislehurst Kent. Coincidentally, the house, although unoccupied, belonged to a Benin man, Efe Inneh. Sato was sure the man resided in Benin.

Osad had been a little disappointed with the information, though. He did not understand Mystery's relationship with the man and failed to see why she had gone to his house straight after leaving his hotel suite and his bed. She had said her home was in Kent, did it mean she lived with this man? He was likely one of those wealthy Benin men who bought properties abroad to house women they used for sexual gratification.

He did not know what was going on, and what Mystery's involvement with the man was, but once his coronation was over, he intended to find Efe Inneh and quiz him thoroughly regarding Mystery. For now, he had to focus. Mostly, things were going according to plan. The redecoration of the kings and queens' quarters in the Oba's palace was finished. Eki had been extremely helpful supervising the work along with his sisters while he hosted countless traditional ceremonies that were a necessary part of his ascension to the throne.

He was dressed and pacing the living room of his quarters when Edosa Aihie entered. He announced that Eki had arrived was being led to the central State Room. Osad thanked him and flanked by the omuadas bearing the royal sceptres of the Ada and Eben, he exited his apartment and walked through the halls in the direction of the State Room. It was packed full of royal family members and high-level chiefs who were present to join him in receiving his bride.

As he entered with pomp and pageantry, he spotted her standing at the far end of the room. His uncle was at her side, waiting to walk her to him. She looked so beautiful he felt his body rouse with excitement and anticipation, and he called upon all his self-control learned over the years from his training to be king and his martial arts practice. His body would not dictate to him. He would dictate to his body.

He halted in the middle of the room, aware of the eyes that were on him as he watched his bride approach him, leaning on his uncle's arm for support. As they reached him, his uncle took her hand and placed it in his, concluding the marriage rites. They were now man and wife according to the Benin native law and customs. The guests rose to their feet, and Chief Isekhure pronounced a blessing on the royal couple to which all that were present, chorused, "*Ise.*"

He lifted her veil and lowered his head to kiss her. Then he froze. That fragrance. It was familiar. It was the same fragrance Mystery had been wearing that night. His body stirred, and he quieted it, using all his will power. He wanted to put back her veil and disappear. This was going to be a lot harder than he had thought. He did not want to sleep with this woman. He reckoned it would be easier to put her away if he did not touch her. The rate he was going, though, he would be crawling into her bed before the night was over.

Focus, Osad. Don't be a fool. Think of Mystery. She is the one that you want.

He realised that the guests watched him, waiting to see him kiss his wife for the first time. He bent his head, evading her mouth and planted a kiss on her cheek, close enough to fool observers into thinking he had kissed her chastely on the mouth.

There was a roar of excitement, and he smiled, pleased with himself. He had done well thus far. If he continued along the same path, he would be putting her away soon without tampering with her virginity. Yes, everything was going according to plan. Soon, Mystery would be here standing before him, and Eki Alile would be history. Well, he corrected himself, she was no longer Eki Alile, she was now Her Royal Highness Princess Eki Edoni. Tomorrow she would be Queen Eki and whatever surname he would pick at his coronation. He took her by the hand and led her away from the hall, amidst cheers from the crowd.

He led her to the bridal chamber where her maids were waiting to prepare her for him. He handed her to the maids and disappeared to his room. The omuadas were waiting to get him undressed and into his pyjamas. If circumstances were different, if she were the woman he wanted, he would use the connecting door that separated their bed chambers and go to her for the night. Things were, however, complicated, and she was not the woman his heart craved so they would be sleeping in separate beds, tonight and every night until their sham of a marriage was terminated.

"Oh, my goodness! You look divine, Eki," Orobosa stated as she entered the bridal chamber even before the maids began to attend to Eki.

"Your Highness," Eki curtsied, smiling politely. "How lovely to see you again."

"Oh, please don't curtsy to me. You are family, and besides as we are all now highnesses, I think it's best we dispense with the titles and simply go by our first names. It makes life easier for everyone."

"Tell me about it," Eki said, and they both shared a giggle.

Orobosa hugged her. "I won't keep you. I only wanted to say welcome to the family."

"Thank you," Eki responded beaming.

"Orobosa, why didn't you tell us you were coming

to see Her Highness?" Ivie asked as she entered the chamber and gasped as she took in the large bed dressed in the finest white silk sheets, the lit scented candles, rose petals strewn across the bed and floor and not to mention the champagne, strawberries and chocolates that adorned the coffee table. She winked mischievously at Eki. "Wow. It looks like my brother is going to keep you up all night, Eki."

Eki and Orobosa giggled uncontrollably. "Yeah, I know what you mean." Orobosa agreed. "The way he was looking at her a moment ago, reminded me of how Edosa looks at me when he wants to have sex."

Eki didn't know what to make of that, and thankfully she was saved from commenting as Omo and Ewere chose that moment to enter the chamber.

"Why are you two here?" Ewere chided. "This is neither the time nor place to offer your congratulations. Osad will soon be here, and she is not ready for him. I warn you; he will be displeased."

"True that," Omo said. "I am going to offer my

congratulations and be gone." She moved closer and embraced Eki. "Congratulations, darling. Welcome to our family, we're so pleased to have you."

"Thank you, Omo."

Ewere also embraced her. "Welcome to the family, Eki. We are certain that you are perfect for our brother."

"Thank you, Ewere."

"Okay, ladies. Let's allow her maids to prepare her." Ewere turned to leave, pulling Ivie and Orobosa with her. Ivie moved away and came forward to embrace Eki.

"I am the only one who hasn't hugged you," she said, causing Ewere to roll her eyes.

"Begs the question what have you been doing?"

Ivie ignored her as she squeezed Eki. "You take good care of that boy, you hear?" she whispered into her ear. "He can be obstinate, but he has a good heart. And we have trained him well. He will make you a fine husband."

Eki fought back the tears that gathered in her eyes. The man she had met in London, the man she had fallen in love with, was a good man. She was sure of that. As for the man she had married, she did not know what to make of him. She was willing to be a good wife and would give anything to get back the man she had been with that night at The Dorchester.

Osad's sisters hurried from the room, and the maids went to work, undressing her, and removing her makeup, and freeing her hair for a comfortable night's sleep. They rushed her into the ensuite bathroom for a quick luxurious bath after which she was massaged and dressed in the sexiest nightwear she had ever set eyes on. It was a beautiful lace-trimmed cami and short set made from pure silk. Her bed was turned down, and she climbed in, waiting for her husband to join her.

As she lay in the large bed with luxurious sheets, she stared at the rings on her finger. They must have cost him a small fortune, and she wondered why he had gone to all the trouble. She supposed it was more an exhibition of his wealth than a display of his affections. Owen may have had some feelings for Mystery, but it was clear that Osad cared nothing for Eki. Those were her thoughts as she listened to the music and voices from the party downstairs in the grounds of the palace that filtered through to her. She closed her eyes and relaxed, and it wasn't long before she was asleep.

Eki could not tell how long she lay before rising from the bed and walking towards the connecting door that linked the bridal chamber to his bedroom. He had not come to her so she would go to him. She hesitated but only briefly. She remembered Orobosa saying Osad had looked at Eki the same way her husband, Edosa Aihie, looked at her when he wanted sex. Boldened by those words, she opened the door and entered the dimly lit bedroom. The only light came from a bedside lamp. Osad lay in the bed, fast asleep. He looked the same way he had when she had last seen him at the hotel in London. His even breathing was the only sound in the room. She approached the bed quietly so as not to rouse him.

Her heart was thumping in her chest with every step that she took.

Osad knew the moment the figure reached him. She had come to him when he had refused to go to her. He had known she was bold, but surely, she was not so bold as to enter his bedroom uninvited.

"Bearding the lion in his den, Eki?" he asked, rolling over on his side to face her.

His eyes snapped open at once, and the sleep disappeared as soon as he saw her. Tonight, she wore a black lace kimono robe. Her eye makeup had been replaced with a black lace eye mask, but she wore her hair in the same ponytail style.

"Mystery?"

He could not believe his good fortune. How had she gained entrance into his room, though? How did she get past the palace guards? Granted the guards at the Edaiken palace were less than those in the Oba's palace but he was close to his coronation and security had increased around him. Anyway, none of that mattered. He had been looking for her, and here she was.

"Where have you been? I have been searching for you."

"I was here the whole time, my love," she responded, much to his pleasure.

"Come here," he ordered, holding out a hand to her. "I want you in my bed."

She took his hand, allowing him to pull her onto the bed. He wrapped his arms around her and vowed silently that now he had her in his arms, he would never let her go again. He had been careless once, and she had left without so much as a goodbye while he slept. He would not be careless again. First, he had to know who she was. He had to know her without the mask.

"Take off your mask, baby. I want to see you." He reached for the mask, but she shook her head and prevented him.

"No," she protested and would have pulled away from him, but he tightened his hold.

"Why not?" he queried.

"I fear that you will reject me," she explained, her voice was faltering.

"I could never reject you," he assured her. He cradled her face in his hands even as he rained soft kisses on every inch of the beautiful skin that was uncovered by the mask. "You were mine from the moment I laid eyes on you." He reached out a second time to remove the mask, and this time she did not stop him, but there was a flicker of sadness in her eyes as his hand pulled the mask off. It tore at his heart.

As the mask came off, Osad found himself staring at a face that had become familiar in the last few weeks. It was not Mystery, after all. It was Eki, playing tricks on him.

"The gods forbid!" he roared as he jumped out of his sleep, drenched in sweat.

CHAPTER NINE

The following morning Eki awakened to the realisation that her husband had rejected her. He had not visited the bridal chamber, and she had slept all alone. She told herself that it did not matter, but she knew it did.

It mattered.

It wrenched her heart.

She shifted in the bed and looked from his vacant place beside her to the connecting door that separated them. She knew he was awake and would be surrounded by the omuadas dressing him in his kingly attire for his coronation. She turned her focus to the tasks of the day as her head maid, Yuki, entered the chamber with two other palace maids in tow.

These maids were different from the ones who had worked with Yuki last night to prepare her. She knew without being told they were here to help her dress, and she sat up, threw back the covers and began to climb out of bed. Once again, she would endure torture as her hair was pulled in all directions to make her look like a Benin queen. She shuddered. She would never get used to the traditional Benin dressing.

"Good morning, Your Highness," Yuki greeted and curtsied. Her companions did not speak, but they curtsied with their heads bowed and kept their eyes averted from the woman who, in a few hours, would be their new queen.

"Good morning, Yuki," Eki greeted, sounding more cheerful than she felt. "Good morning, ladies," she addressed the two maids who looked at each other in surprise and curtsied again in acknowledgement. Their behaviour didn't surprise Eki. She knew from her time with Oba Edoni that palace servants were deaf, blind, and mute. Not literally but they were trained to be as inconspicuous as possible. Eki knew these maids would not be speaking to her and would leave all the talking to

Yuki, her head maid.

"Did you have a good night's sleep, Your Highness?" Yuki asked as she waved the maids into the bathroom to prepare Eki's bath.

Was it her imagination, or did the girl's smile increase ever so slightly as she asked the question?

Cheeky burger, Eki thought.

I slept well, thank you." As she walked away from the bed, she noticed that Yuki's eyes hurriedly scanned the white sheets. It was quick and discreet, but Eki was no fool. She knew exactly what was going on here. If the young girl were hoping to see bloodstains, she would be disappointed. Eki considered for the first time what the poor maid who removed Osad's sheets at The Dorchester Hotel had thought. Those sheets had been stained with her blood. The absence of blood on these sheets was not the only evidence the soon to be king had not slept with his wife. The unwrinkled pillows on the side of the bed that should have been his were a dead giveaway.

That's your evidence right there, Yuki. Make what you want of it, Eki thought as she walked towards the bathroom and the maids who had run her bath and were waiting for her.

Later that morning, they departed for the Oba's palace. Osad walked on foot, as tradition dictated, from Uselu where the palace of the Edaiken of Uselu was situated to the king's square, in the city centre, where the Oba's palace was located, and where the throne of his ancestors awaited him. It was a journey a little more than five miles and ahead of him were the traditional dancers who performed the customary ritual of cleansing the ground upon which the soon to be king trod. Eki rode alone in a white Rolls Royce Phantom that bore the royal sceptres of the Ada and Eben on the number plates.

The roads through which they travelled had been lined from the breaking of dawn with people old and young who had come out to catch a glimpse of their new Oba and his Oloi. Many of them were dressed in attires made of fabric showcasing the photograph of the new Oba. Indeed, across the city, banners, billboards, and flags, bearing the crown prince's portrait, were visible. Hundreds of Benin people in the diaspora had flown in to witness this once-in-a-lifetime event. Members of royal families from across the length and breadth of Africa and Europe had also flown into Benin to commemorate the ascension of Prince Osad Edoni to the Benin throne. As could be imagined, the local police officers had their hands full maintaining law and order amidst the jubilations. There was also the problem of traffic all over the city which had to be managed before it reached gridlock.

As the procession moved on, the crowds cheered and waved their flags, and Eki found herself in awe at the love of the Benin people for their monarch. She was also awed that she was part of the monarchy and that although she was beginning the journey as Princess Eki Edoni, she would finish it as Queen Eki. Her surname would change from Edoni to whatever surname Osad would choose for himself before the coronation ceremony was over. As tradition dictated, he would not mount the throne with the name his father had used to reign.

Osad was at liberty to choose the same name, but that would make him Oba Edoni II. His grandfather had been Oba Ezoti II, and his father picked the name Edoni and became Oba Edoni I. Today Osad would choose his name. As he walked towards the Oba's palace, he would make a brief stop at Useh where he would pick the name with which he would reign as king. Eki hoped that, like his father who had picked a new name and thus became Oba Edoni I, Osad would choose a new name. A new name for a fresh start, that was the way it was to be.

She lowered her eyes and looked at the rings on her fingers. As she toyed with them, she thought again of the night before. Why had he not come to her? Did he not want her? If he didn't, why marry her in the first place? There were many girls presented to him, why her? And if he didn't want her, why did he spend all this money and go beyond the call of duty to ensure she had everything she desired? It made no sense.

Moreover, Orobosa had mentioned that Osad had looked at Eki the way her husband looked at her when he wanted sex. She had reasons to believe the other woman was right. When Osad had lifted her veil, and just before he kissed her, he had looked at her as though he wanted to rip her clothes off. He had looked at Mystery the same way that unforgettable night at The Dorchester. Then, afterwards, he had handed her to her maids to prepare her for the bridal night and never showed.

Who did that? she wondered and sighed. She was overthinking this. Maybe he had been tired; after all, he had been hosting countless traditional festivals during the last two weeks or so. Conceivably he was preoccupied with his coronation activities and did not want to be distracted.

Yes, that must be it. He did not want to be distracted.

Osad was distracted.

He had not slept a wink after that dream last night. He had stayed up thinking about Eki and Mystery, and the next thing he knew, the omuadas were at his door to help him bathe and get dressed. Even while they attended to him, his eyes kept going to the connecting door that separated him from her. It had taken every ounce of willpower he possessed not to send the omuadas away and go to her. His desire to have her was driving him out of his mind. This was a whole new experience for him.

Granted, he was an extremely busy man and had a brief attention span, which meant that his relationships had never lasted long, but while they lasted, he had eyes only for the woman he was with. He did not spend time lusting after another woman. And while sex with his previous girlfriends had been good, he had never felt this intense need to be with a woman; it was a need that threatened to make him lose reason.

What had come over him? First, he took a stranger to his bed and poured his seed into her. He had never done that before; never given any woman his seed. His father's warning had followed him everywhere, and he had taken extra precautions to ensure it never happened. Then he met Mystery, and even though he had no idea who she genuinely was, he succumbed to the heat of the moment, acting foolishly. Now, she was gone, and likely belonged to the man called Efe Inneh.

Where did that leave him? Where did that leave them? More importantly, why had she come to him? Did she know who he was? If she was involved with a Benin man, was it not likely she had easily identified him despite his being incognito? Had she been used to set him up? If so, for what purpose? Indeed, if that had been the case, surely Sato would have discovered it? And suppose she had conceived his child; a royal heir while being tied to this Efe Inneh? As if that was not trouble enough to make his ancestors turn in their graves, he was lusting after a woman he had refused to marry, to begin with.

Was he going to sleep with her?

Give her his seed?

Make her pregnant?

What happened when Mystery turned up and pregnant? No, he was not going to complicate issues. Mystery may have abandoned him the morning after, but until he saw her and knew what was going on and where their relationship stood, he was not going to get involved with Eki.

What was he thinking?

He wouldn't get involved with her at all. She would be his wife only in name; he planned to put her away untouched, and that was what he was going to do. He would need all the self-control he had garnered over the years, but it would be worth it. He was not going to mess up his life any more than he already had.

He pushed her out of his mind and focused on the road ahead. The sun was starting to come up and walking in the heat, and under the layers of traditional coral beads and beaded garments was exhausting. The coral beads alone weighed 20 kilos. How he was expected to lift himself under that weight was beyond him. Even leaning on the arms of the chiefs who escorted him, he felt weary. He longed for the day's activities to be over so that he could crawl into bed and cram several nights' worth of sleep into one night.

Once again, his mind drifted to Eki, and he wondered if she was okay and if she had everything she needed. He knew she was in one of the many cars that followed behind the multitude of chiefs and palace guards that walked with him on foot. Her car would be first in convoy. He thought about how beautiful she had looked last night, and he wondered what she was wearing today and if she looked as beautiful. He desired to turn around in the hopes of seeing her; he longed for a glimpse of her.

Osad, behave, he warned and drudged on.

The shrine in Useh came into view just then, and he smiled. He would rest there a bit while he picked a new name. The rest was a welcome development. The crowd on foot and the cars in the procession paused outside as he entered the shrine with only a handful of the chiefs who had escorted him.

Chief Isekhure in his role as the chief priest was waiting for him and welcomed him before leading him to the hall that bore the staffs of office belonging to his ancestors, with some dating back more than four hundred years. The process was short and straight to the point. He followed the priest's directions, and when it was time to pick a name, he rejected the names of the Obas that had preceded him and chose a name that had never been used before.

"Ehigie," he declared when the Chief Priest asked what name he preferred.

Chief Isekhure bowed his head in acknowledgement, thus bringing that part of the ceremony to an end.

He departed from Useh as he continued his journey towards the Oba's palace to mount the throne of his fathers. He would reign as Oba Ehigie I of the Benin Kingdom. Once again, his mind drifted to Eki. She would now be known as Queen Eki Ehigie. He hoped she liked her new surname.

Where did that come from? he marvelled.

Focus, boy, he admonished himself.

He entered the palace through the north gate. Ahead of him in the massive open courtyard of the north wing stood the throne of his ancestors, and next to the throne were the members of the Uzama; the kingmakers, all six of them. Coincidentally as crown prince and Edaiken of Uselu he had been the seventh member of the Uzama. When he ascended the throne in a few minutes, he would cease to be a kingmaker and that position would be reserved for his heir who would become the next crown prince and Edaiken of Uselu.

As he approached, Chief Usi Isekhure, who was also a member of the Uzama, led the six members of the Uzama towards him. Behind Chief Isekhure was Chief Edosa Aihie, and four other members of the

Uzama. The chiefs who had journeyed with him thus far stood back as he was received and escorted by the kingmakers towards the throne.

In a matter of minutes, it was all done; he was on the throne, the crown was placed on his head by a member of the Uzama and the omuadas who bore the royal sceptres and who had walked with him from the Edaiken's palace, now moved and took their place behind him to the right and left-hand sides of the throne.

Chief Usi Isekhure to whom he had mentioned his name at the shrine in Useh, uttered it for the first time and before the people gathered.

"*Omo N'Oba N'Edo Uku-akpolokpolo Oba Ehigie I of the Benin Kingdom!*" he cried as he formally introduced the new monarch to the kingdom. Instantly all six members of the Uzama faced him, raised their fists, and saluted. Then went up another cry from Chief Isekhure.

"*Oba gha to kpèré.*"

And all who had gathered, even those in the

streets, shouted, "*Ise!*"

"Long live the king," Isekhure concluded.

"Your Majesty, it is time."

Eki looked up at her head maid who had entered the sitting hall where she had been waiting patiently since arriving at the palace. She had not been allowed into the courtyard and had instead been shown to this reception room where members of her family had taken turns to sit with her and apprise her of the goings-on in the courtyard. Tiyan named every single African royal father and mother in attendance. According to her, she had even spotted members of the royal families of Europe, and she was already reeling off names when Yuki entered and interrupted them. Not that Eki had been listening to Tiyan's tirade anyway. Her head was filled with essential matters such as her marriage and the future and had no room left to bother with who exactly was present for the coronation ceremony of her new husband.

She frowned slightly. Had Osad been crowned? Already? Surely, if she was now being referred to as your majesty. Until now the girl had addressed her as your highness.

"Has His Highness been…?"

Before she finished the girl, Yuki smiled and interrupted her. "The crown prince is now *Omo N'Oba N'Edo Uku-akpolopolo Oba Ehigie I of the Benin Kingdom*," she said with enthusiasm.

Eki understood her excitement. Indeed, the excitement of all Benin people, many of whom were grateful to be alive to witness this once-in-a-lifetime event. How many Benin people got to see two kings mount the throne in their lifetime? It called for all the exhilaration one could muster.

"Yippee! You are now the queen!" An excited Tiyan leapt to her feet, walked over to where Eki sat and threw her arms around her. "Congratulations, Your Majesty."

Eki smiled faintly in response. She would have been enthused herself except that she felt like a fraud. Osad did not love her and that stung. She longed for the man he had been the first night she had met him. She marvelled that he was so different now and why. She concluded that he wasn't different; it was merely that he revealed his unpleasant side to her because he did not want her.

As Eki rose, a host of women, palace maids, emerged from within the palace to escort her. Tiyan took that as her cue to leave and join the rest of the family outside in the courtyard. Yuki led the queen's procession. Slowly but gracefully, they made their way towards the square where Oba Ehigie sat on the throne surrounded by prominent chiefs and illustrious sons and daughters of the kingdom, security personnel, and of course pressmen who were photographing the newly coronated king. They hurriedly dispersed, making way for the queen and her entourage.

Osad drew in his breath sharply as Eki appeared,

and he felt his body stir in response to her presence. The woman had a way of eliciting a reaction from him against his wishes. And his body seemed to have a mind of its own and did not do as it was told. He watched as the maids ushered her towards his left-hand side to take her place next to him on the throne that had been made especially for her. He had ordered it for her. It was not the same one his mother used. Now that he thought about it, he wondered why he had done that when he did not plan to keep her as his wife. She was only a means to an end. She had always been exactly that to him, although as he watched her now, he knew he was kidding himself.

He found her desirable; the way she walked demurely, the way she paused before him to curtsy alongside her maidservants, and the way she lowered her eyes and kept them to the ground. She was the epitome of submission, and it aroused in him a desire to make her his, a desire to love her and support her and protect her. Not that he thought her to be as demure as she looked. He knew she was feisty, a proper honey badger. He remembered the day at the Edaiken's palace when she had not cowered but had knocked down the statue of the king. He smiled at the memory. Her impudence both challenged and thrilled him.

As she sat on her throne next to his, he noticed that she mirrored his actions, and at the same time as he did, she produced a handkerchief and placed it over her mouth. It was a sign that as king and queen, Oba and Oloi, their words conveyed authority, and thus, while they were quick to hear, they were slow to speak.

That's my girl, he thought and instantly rebuked himself.

Behave Ehigie. Behave.

For the next hour dignitaries who had come to witness the coronation ceremony filed past them bowing in obeisance to the new king and queen of the Benin Kingdom..

CHAPTER TEN

One week after the coronation, the festivities had dwindled, and life began to return to normal. The traffic gradually reduced as dignitaries who had travelled from all over the world to Benin to witness the coronation ceremony departed to their respective nations. Only that morning, Osad's sisters had returned to London. Eki was sad to see them go, and she made them promise to visit soon, and they were able to extract a similar promise from her.

She was fully settled in her new home, the queen's quarters, and settling into her role as queen and the work that came with it. The Oloi's office was at the centre and crucial to the smooth running of the citadel. She discovered that meant all the palaces and stately homes belonging to the Oba of Benin both in Benin and abroad. Her duty as queen went beyond managing the budget for the running of the castles. It included hosting parties and visiting royalty and other dignitaries. There was also the welfare of staff and their families which was handled by her office.

In the week that followed the coronation, her office was engaged with arranging piles of wedding and coronation presents. The guests had undoubtedly gone to town bestowing favours on the new king and queen, because never in her life had she seen so many gifts. She worked with her chief of staff, personal assistant and head maid, Yuki to sort through the pile. Occasionally other maids from the palace joined them, and the gifts had finally been organised and filled one of the great rooms in the palace. She had no idea what to do with them all. She would have to discuss this with Osad. And that was another problem.

Osad, or Oba Ehigie, as he was now fondly called by all and sundry, was drifting even further away. He hosted parties and traditional festivals, and even though the king's quarters were next to the queen's residence and there was a secret passage from the king's bedroom straight into the queen's bedroom, Eki seldom saw him. Therefore, discussing anything with him proved difficult.

Sometimes she found herself wondering what he was up to and whether when he did not come to her at night, he was all by himself or if he visited the harem in the west wing. She knew that although Oba Edoni's concubines had previously occupied the harem, they had been relocated to other homes outside the palace. In their place, the harem was crowded with young girls. During the coronation ceremony, many young girls were brought to the harem by their ambitious fathers who hoped to use their daughters to benefit from the king.

Who could blame them? Osad was not only politically influential but also the wealthiest king who had ever sat on the Benin throne. Eki did not want to think of Osad going to another woman's bed. It tore her heart to shreds, but what could she do? She was here now. She had sought to escape this life by running to London and throwing herself at a man who would take her virginity. With her rotten luck, that man turned out to be the same man she was running from. The joke was on her.

She dismissed thoughts of him from her mind. What did it matter whether he was paying her any attention or not? As queen, she had enough palace business to keep her engaged. Since the coronation ended last weekend, she had been up every morning before sunrise and in bed well after midnight. Besides, she had finally floated her company, Elevate, together with Amenze and Tiyan. It had been her dream while they had been on the MBA course in London to start the company.

The vision was to connect young Benin men and women with business ideas with wealthy Benin investors at home and in the diaspora. This week, Amenze, who had been tasked with registering the company formally, had done so. This afternoon, they were meeting at Aiai's home to discuss Elevate with Aiai and Efe.

Efe had gone abroad on business the day after the coronation and had returned last night. They hoped to secure his support as an investor for Elevate. Eki was confident that if he backed the business, he would introduce them to a long list of potential investors who would be interested in investing in the business ideas of their prospective clients. After all, he built homes for the rich. If anyone could introduce them to the rich with idle money to invest, it was him. She knew Osad's influence would be substantial, but she couldn't ask him to come on board. He did not care for her as a wife; why would he care about her dreams?

To him, she was simply the daughter of Alile, one of the poorest palace chiefs in the kingdom. Maybe if her father had been wealthy like Chief Ezomo, she would have had his attention. The problem in their marriage centred on his pride and prejudice. She was not from the same social strata as he was; therefore, he paid her no attention. She was inconsequential to him. It had been a week and a day since they married, and they had not shared a meal, let alone a bed. He clearly did not want her, which begged the question, why had he married her?

She had no answers to the questions in her heart but refused to let Osad or his blatant rejection of her dampen her spirits. With Yuki's help, she got dressed quickly; she did not want to be late. She was beginning to learn to move around incognito. She did not wish palace guards, maids, or police officers to follow her everywhere she went. As many people had only seen her from a distance or on television during the coronation, she reckoned she could get away with going out incognito in Benin.

Once she was dressed, Yuki wanted to know if she should call the palace garage and ask for a car to be brought to the front door for Eki. She considered the question for a minute as she contemplated what car she wanted to drive. She knew there were many exotic cars in the palace. The vehicles belonging to Oba Edoni were parked in the palace garage in the east wing, and besides, a good number of Osad's cars had been moved from the Edaiken's palace.

It would be the first time she would drive herself since being married to Osad. Although she had recently taken delivery of a red Rolls Royce Cullinan which Osad informed her was her wedding present, she decided to annoy him by driving his brand-new Bentley Mulsanne. He had taken delivery of the vehicle at the same time she had taken delivery of the Cullinan, and he was yet to drive it apart from test driving it around the palace grounds. He would be livid, and he would not be able to resist coming over and telling her what he thought of her behaviour.

The thought excited Eki. She told Yuki to ring the garage and ask a driver to bring the Bentley up to her front door. After less than a minute, Yuki turned to Eki and informed her that the person at the other end of the line said it was the king's car and there were specific instructions that no one else was to drive it.

Eki hid a smile as she took the phone. Without waiting for the person on the other end to speak, she said, "This is Oloi Eki. Deliver the car to my front door now. If the king asks, tell him I requested for the car. I am his wife; I can drive any of his cars I choose."

She hung up the phone, and in minutes, the car was delivered to her doorsteps. She slid in behind the wheels and exited the palace through the south gate.

If this doesn't get his attention, then nothing will, she mused as she sped towards Aiai and Efe's home.

Osad sat in the office inside the king's apartment finishing a video conference call with vice presidents of his company when Usi and Edosa entered. Although Orobosa had returned home to London that morning, Edosa was hanging on for one more week to help Osad with the transition following his coronation. As it was Saturday, he had promised both men a game of golf followed by lunch at the golf club, and he was looking forward to it.

The recreation facility was one of several owned by his father's company in Benin, Crown Group, and

Osad enjoyed using it every time he had the opportunity. Not that it was often. Spending time with his childhood buddies at the club today was his way of unwinding as the festivities following the coronation were coming to an end.

"Hey, Osad. What's up? Still up for golf?" Usi asked as he dropped into the chair opposite the desk.

Osad looked up from his laptop and scowled. "Will you address me properly? *Ozuwo*!"

Both men chuckled, and he smiled.

"I have warned him to be respectful," Edosa said and slapped Usi behind the head. Osad laughed out loud.

"Thank you, Edosa. I have been itching to do that all week."

"Oh?" Usi asked feigning surprise. "Have I annoyed you that much? Here I thought my performance was outstanding."

"It was. You were exceptional during the coronation and afterwards. Your father would have been proud. Even so, I wanted to smack your head." He shrugged and added, "Just because I can."

"Yeah, I know that feeling," Edosa agreed and slapped Usi's head again.

"Ouch! Stop it already! Show some respect for my office. I am the chief priest of the kingdom and the head of all palace chiefs, which makes me your boss."

"Yes, boss," Edosa sneered and then turned to Osad. "Say, Osad, we are yet to go for a spin in your newly delivered Bentley."

"You will today," Osad assured him. "If you're happy to leave your cars here we can take the Bentley up to the golf course and back." He looked from one man to the other.

Both shrugged. "Sounds like a plan," Usi said.

Osad pushed the button on his desk, and an omuada entered the office.

"Ask a palace driver to fetch my Bentley Mulsanne from the garage and bring it up to the front door."

The man disappeared and was back within a few minutes, bowing as he entered.

"My lord, I was informed that the queen went out in the Bentley."

Osad frowned. "In my new Mulsanne? I am the only one authorised to drive that car."

Bowing and averting the king's eyes, the man responded. "My lord, I understand that Her Majesty was dissuaded, and another vehicle offered, but she insisted on the Bentley saying that she is your wife and therefore entitled to drive any of your cars."

Osad turned slowly to look at Usi and Edosa, an incredulous look upon his face. Both men equally had incredulous looks on their faces, and together they burst out laughing.

They left for the golf course in another car, and while Osad struggled to be in the moment, and enjoy his time with his friends, his mind kept drifting to Eki.

Where had she gone?

For the first time, it occurred to him that he knew little regarding her, her family, and the circle she moved in. Like him, she may have been unwilling to enter into this marriage. He had not considered this before now. Did she have a boyfriend who was biding his time, and ready to take her back at a moment's notice? He recalled Usi had mentioned Ezomo's son wanting to marry her. Usi also said the young man had married her sister. Had she moved on and was there another man in her life that no one knew about? Was that where she had gone? Was this man touching her, kissing her, making love to her, while Osad played golf with his buddies?

The thought stayed with him all through the golf session and lunch. They retired to the palace to watch a game of football in his residence. On arrival, he was notified that Chief Ezomo was waiting in one of the guest houses in the west wing, with his daughter; the daughter who resided in America and who he wanted Osad to meet. She had only just returned.

Osad sat through the ordeal of a meeting while Edosa and Usi waited in his house for his return. It didn't take him long to decipher that Chief Ezomo planned to leave his daughter in the harem. And why not? He was aware that other chiefs had done this, and that the harem was currently filled with beautiful young women whose fathers hoped Osad would sleep with them, thus causing them to become queen or concubine. Some were even happy for their daughters to be love slaves, existing only to satisfy the king's sexual needs, provided they remained in the palace.

Osad thought it was revolting and he was finding the entire business of being introduced to a woman or more each day exhausting. He even forgot their names before they left his presence. He was determined to fix the problem soon. He could ask Eki for help, after all, the office of the Oloi catered to the needs of the harem.

Are you insane? The harem is what you need to remind

her that you do not want her. How can you get rid of it? And you want her to help you? Focus, Ehigie. It is Mystery you want. You are going to get rid of Eki soon.

He pulled out his phone to text Sato. He wanted an update on Mystery and Efe Inneh. Sato had been busy during the coronation, but since it was over, he should have gone back to the task of finding Efe Inneh. As he began to text, instead of asking for an update on Mystery, he found himself asking the other man to place the queen under surveillance. He wanted to know where she went, who she saw, what they did or discussed.

If he discovered that there was a man somewhere touching his wife or waiting to embrace her after he put her away, he was going to take great pleasure in hanging him in the evil forest as his ancestors would have in ancient times. That should serve as a warning that his wife was off-limits. He was the crowned lion, and no hyena was going to play around his lioness.

She is not your lioness, remember? What happens when you find Mystery, the woman you want?

Shut up! Osad silenced the voice inside his head.

"My lord, the king, seems distracted."

Osad looked up from his phone at the woman sitting opposite him, and he narrowed his eyes. He did not like her one bit.

Why is she here again?

"Your daughter is very westernised, Chief Ezomo, she appears to have little or no knowledge of the Benin tradition or how one comports oneself in the presence of the king." He turned to her. "My dear, usually people do not speak in my presence unless in response to a question I pose to them, and they certainly do not speak to me directly unless invited to do so."

Instantly, both father and daughter were on their feet and bowing before him.

"Please, forgive us, Your Majesty." Chief Ezomo said as Osad waved them to be seated.

"Please be seated. You are forgiven. The king has no delight in the destruction of his people," he assured them. The Benin people revered their king and believed that his displeasure in a subject could lead to the individual's devastation.

The girl sat with her head bowed, and Osad saw she was close to tears, but he did not care. He was in a sour mood, and he needed a scapegoat, and she had foolishly presented herself as an easy target. No doubt she came here thinking she had the edge over his wife because her father was the wealthiest chief in the kingdom, and she had been raised in America. How dare she speak to him with such familiarity as though they were lovers? He had not even met her for ten minutes. She needed to learn her place.

Eki left the Bentley in front of the queen's residence for the drivers to return to the garage. She was in a cheerful mood. The afternoon spent with Aiai, and the girls had been eventful. They had delivered an outstanding presentation to Efe, who had been full of questions. But they had been prepared and answered all his questions leaving him in no doubt of their ability to run Elevate successfully. He had announced his willingness to invest, he and Aiai would be buying shares in the business to provide the capital required for take-off. Everything was falling into place; she was elated. As she turned in the direction of her front door, Osad emerged through his front door and began to walk toward her.

"I see you have returned," he said through clenched teeth. Most of his annoyance was directed at himself for wanting her when he should be angry with her for going out without his knowledge and in his car! Plus, she had gone out incognito, no guards, no maids, only God knew what she had got up to.

He was glad he had asked Sato to watch her every move. Going forward, he would be notified of everything she did, when she did it, and with whom.

"I wonder," he continued, "when you go wherever it is that you go without the knowledge, permission, or company of your husband don't these people, whoever they are that you go to see, ask why your husband isn't with you?"

Eki shrugged nonchalantly. "I tell them that my husband and I do not live in each other's pockets," she responded. "It is what you want, isn't it?"

Whatever she meant by that, he refused to let her provoke him. He had ordered eyes on her, and therefore if she were using his distance to nurture advances from other men, he would soon know of it.

"Did you enjoy driving my car?" he asked, instead.

She smiled and turned to look at the car. Aiai and the girls had loved it, and they thought it suited her perfectly. She had taken them for a spin. It had been pure joy.

"It's a sweetheart of a car. I loved driving it," she winked mischievously.

She was flirting with him. Osad realised, and as he

watched her, he felt like he was dying inside. He wanted to kiss that mouth and feel that body next to his. He desired to brand her so that she and everyone else knew who owned her.

Remind me again why you haven't slept with her?

Behave, Ehigie, he warned.

He moved around the car to inspect it for scratches and dents. Eki watched him in amusement.

Men, she thought. *They were all the same.*

He reminded her of her father every time her mother drove his car.

"Satisfied, my liege lord?" she asked as he walked towards her again.

He ignored the sarcasm dripping in her tone. "Fortunately, for you, there are no dents or scratches, or else I would have put you over my knee." The words came out wrong; he realised a little too late.

Eki's eyes widened in astonishment, and the pupils dilated. Her mouth formed an O shape that was quickly replaced with a grin that was saccharine sweet.

"Oh, I do hope that's a promise, my liege," she said in her most flirtatious voice and winked again. Before Osad responded, she turned in the direction of her front door and left him standing in the driveway next to his beloved car; his eyes fixed to her backside. She must have known he was watching her, because she paused, turned around, touched her fingers to her lips, and blew him a kiss in an exaggerated gesture. She laughed and continued her catwalk until she disappeared inside the building.

He was lost instantly; he failed to remember that as Oba, no one turned their back on him or walked away from him. This woman had just done that, and he, like a fool, allowed it and did nothing but watch the swaying of her hips.

He groaned. "Ehigie you are in trouble."

"She will be the death of you. Just take her to bed and be done with it already," Usi said, and Osad turned to see that Usi and Edosa had joined him out on the driveway in front of the queen's house.

He eyed Usi angrily. "Shut your mouth. *Ozuwo!*" he growled. "Did you see how she just walked out on me?" he asked Edosa.

"Mhmm," he responded.

Osad frowned. "Is she supposed to do that?"

Before Edosa answered, Usi said, "Well, no one is permitted to turn their back on the king."

"Then why did she do that? Hasn't she been taught the protocol?"

"Oh, Eki knows the protocol well, Osad. She learnt it first at your father's feet," Usi answered.

"Then, why did she -?"

Edosa patted him on the shoulder. "I think the real question here is why did you let her?"

"Maybe you enjoyed watching the sway of her hips as she walked away?" Usi teased.

Osad turned and scowled, but it was Edosa who smacked Usi behind the head playfully.

"Shut up. *Ozuwo*!" he said..

CHAPTER ELEVEN

A week passed, and they did not see each other, and then the following Saturday morning, he entered the gym to find her there. He knew she used the gym shared by their residences and accessible from the inside of either home. Sometimes he entered and saw tell-tale signs that she had been there. But thus far, he was yet to share the space with her.

Today, it seemed, they were going to inhabit the room together. She was running on the treadmill dressed in a pair of blue motion seamless leggings and a matching crop top that left her mid rift and a good portion of her back bare, and it was more than Osad could do not to stand and gawk at her perfect body. She caught his eye in the mirror, and he snapped out of his reverie and moved away from her.

"Good morning," he mumbled grouchily.

"Good morning, my liege lord," Eki responded, panting as she did. "You're as grumpy as a bear with a sore head this morning. What's the matter? Didn't you sleep well last night? Or are you not a morning person?"

"If you aim to goad me, I have news for you. I came to work out in silence." He fixed her a stony stare.

"Okay," Eki panted and chuckled at the same time. "No need to be grumpy."

For a while, they worked out in silence each keeping as far away from the other as possible. Then Eki watched in amazement as he went through a black belt kata. Until this morning, when he had entered the gym wearing a black gi, she had had no idea he was a martial artist. She was reminded of when as an undergraduate she had joined the karate team at her university. She had risen quickly to the brown belt being passionate about the sport. However, preparing for her bar exams immediately after graduation meant she had to discontinue training. Her mother had been glad; she had not once encouraged her love of sports. When Eki had been a short distance sprinter on her secondary school team, it had been a problem. When she joined the Shotokan karate team in her university, all hell had been let loose. Her mother had told her repeatedly that no man would marry her.

She watched Osad with nostalgia, as one after the other, her friends who had been blackbelt holders appeared in her mind's eye performing the kata. He finished paused and started a new kata. She instantly identified it as Bassai Dai; it was the last kata she had perfected before discontinuing training. She fell in line behind him and moved with him. It was amazing how much she remembered. When it was over, she was smiling, and surprisingly, so was he.

"Where did you learn to do Bassai Dai?" he asked, amazed once again by this woman before him.

"I used to be with the Shotokan karate team in my school as an undergrad. I went up to the brown belt, and it was the last kata I perfected before leaving," she replied. "And you?"

"I have been doing karate since my undergrad

days. I am currently a first dan black belt. I've been too busy to grade in the last three years. Bassai Dai is my favourite kata."

"Do you want to do it again?" she asked.

He laughed. "Sure. Why not?"

This time, they stood side by side, and she gave the command to begin. "Hajime!" Together they started to move in unison as though they were one person. He loved it.

As he left the gym, he considered how alike they were and how much he still didn't know about her. He wished for the first time that things had been different, that he had met her when his father had asked him to. She was nothing like he had imagined and if he had given her half a chance, they would have been happy together, but he hadn't, and things were not only different, they were currently also complicated. Mystery was out there carrying his baby, and he still wanted her, despite how much he wished to hold on to Eki. It was total insanity and confusion.

What was he going to do?

Later that evening, he was in one of the guest houses, entertaining visitors who continued to visit him with never-ending requests now that he was king. He felt his phone vibrate and pulled it out of his pocket. It was a call from Sato. He excused himself and entered a vacant reception room.

"Yes, Sato. Talk to me," he ordered and paced the room.

This had better be good.

"Good evening, Your Majesty. I thought you should know that I have found Efe Inneh, and the girl, Mystery."

He halted. "Where?"

"Right here in Benin. I'm at *After-Midnight*, on Central Road and they are both here."

Osad knew *After-Midnight*; it was a high-class night club and bar reserved for the top echelons of Benin. It was the sort of place the rich frequented to see other rich folk and discuss business.

"Bring her to me," he instructed.

The woman had some questions to answer, as did Efe Inneh. For now, he was willing to let Efe Inneh off the hook unless he discovered that the fellow had touched his woman.

"That won't be a good idea, Your Majesty. I think you should come here and see her for yourself."

"Sato, I said bring her to me, even if you have to carry her physically."

"But, Your Majesty – "

"Oh, for the love of God!" he snapped impatiently. "Stay where you are, I am on my way. You better make sure she doesn't disappear before I get there."

He arrived at the club with a single bodyguard, and Sato was waiting outside to escort him inside. He hoped he would not be recognised and kept his head down and avoided eye contact as he made his way through the crowds towards the VIP area where Sato had spotted the girl and Efe Inneh.

To enable him to get a better view, Sato took him upstairs, and as he stood in the gallery, Sato pointed to the level below them where he promptly identified Mystery. She was dressed in the same way she had been that night at The Dorchester in London.

She sat on a stool by the bar backing him, and a tall man stood by her and appeared to be intrigued with whatever she was saying. Then he leaned forward and spoke close to her ear, to be heard above the loud music playing in the background. Whatever he told her must have delighted her because she leapt off the bar stool animatedly and embraced him. He laughed and hugged her and, at that moment, Osad felt a combination of jealousy and fury rise within him. He would have that man's head on a platter!

He made to move, but Sato prevented him.

"Your Majesty, please take a closer look at her," he encouraged.

Osad frowned. What the hell was he supposed to be looking for? He didn't have to ask Sato because at that moment a slim tall woman he recognised as Eki's older sister, joined the couple. Behind her were two other girls he was sure had come with Chief Alile to his palace the day Eki was formally introduced to him. Usi had been ogling one of them. They had also escorted her to the Edaiken's palace the day she was presented to him as his bride. All three women were present except Eki. His frown deepened, and he turned to Sato who was looking at him.

"Where is the queen as we speak?" he asked. He refused to believe it even though the answer to his question was right there before him.

"The man with them is Efe Inneh," Sato said instead. "He is married to Her Majesty's older sister."

Osad sighed and pinched the bridge of his nose. He took another look at Mystery hoping against hope that it was not what he thought, not what Sato was insinuating. It was. Take away the ponytail and wash away the eye makeup, and that was Eki right there. Well, that certainly explained why she had reacted in surprise when they met in Benin. He remembered his dream the night of their wedding night, her perfume, the constant glint in her eyes.

Hadn't her playfulness reminded him so much of Mystery?

"Oh, my God!" he groaned.

Eki was Mystery? Why hadn't she said anything? She had been with him the whole time he had been looking for her?

"You asked me to put eyes on the queen. I did just that. I have been watching her all week, following her everywhere and tonight I saw her leave the house wearing the same attire she had worn at The Dorchester. I knew she was the one. Everything came together. When you asked me to bring her, naturally I did not dare. I did not think you wanted me touching Her Royal Majesty that way."

Osad nodded his understanding. His head was reeling. She had been with him the whole time, and he had not known it? How?

It was because he had only seen what he wanted to see. Had it not been his experience, especially in business, that people only saw what they wanted to see?

"I am going over there to meet her. Later, you and I are going to have a chat. I want to know how the woman you were looking for was under your nose the entire time, and you did not know it," he rasped.

Eki was having a good time with her favourite people in the whole world. It was even better because Efe was with them tonight. He hardly ever came out with them, and she was glad that he had tonight. She was also pleased that she had come out dressed as Mystery. That way, she could relax and enjoy herself and not have to worry about someone identifying her as the queen and reporting back to the palace or the press. As they chatted loudly, to be heard over the music, she instantly sensed eyes on her. She instinctively turned her head towards the gallery and froze. She was staring into the eyes of her husband. He was standing with a man she was confident had to be a member of his security detail. From the look on his face, she knew that he had put the puzzle together. He knew Mystery and Eki were the same person, and he did not look best pleased.

"Folks, I need to get out of here." Eki addressed her companions, but her eyes were fixed on Osad, making his way towards the stairs. He was coming downstairs to meet her. Four pairs of eyes followed hers, and they equally froze at the sight of their king walking towards them. Eki did not hang around to see what would become of them. She grabbed her purse and ran through the crowds pushing and shoving her way towards the exit. As she raced, she looked over her shoulder and saw that he continued to follow her. This was not good.

As she stepped outside, she bumped into a man and all but fell. He grabbed her by the arms and steadied her. She looked up to thank him and realised it was Odaro Ezomo.

She gulped. "Odaro!" Eki had not seen him in ages, and she had no idea that he and Eseosa had returned from their honeymoon.

He frowned and halted as he recognised her behind the heavy eye makeup. "Eki?" he asked. He knew nothing of Mystery, so naturally, he was surprised.

"Yes, it is me," she said.

He looked at her in astonishment. It was as though he had not seen her before tonight or dated her for five years for that matter.

"Eki. It's so good to see you again." He put out a hand to caress her face.

"Get your hands off my wife!" Osad bellowed uncaring as to who was around and watching him.

Was that not Ezomo's son he learnt had dated her and was married to her sister? Why was he looking at her like that? Did he not know she was off-limits to him and any other man alive, or did he have a death wish?

Osad was fuming as he approached them. Eki pulled away from Odaro and kept running. Osad walked towards the younger man who was instantly apprehensive. He was going to hit him in the face, but Sato stepped in between them giving the other man a chance to escape.

"May the king live forever." Odaro bowed in obeisance and hurried away.

Osad glowered at Sato before turning to see Mystery climb into a Mercedes Benz sports car he recognised as one of his. If he had any doubt that she was Eki, it was settled here. Eki was Mystery. He knew that without a doubt, but what he was yet to discover was why she had left him and why she had not told him the truth from the beginning.

He climbed into his Bugatti and gave her a hot chase. If she was racing home to undress and jump into bed like she had not been out, she was mistaken. He was hot on her tail and would leave her no such opportunity.

Osad parked the Bugatti behind the Mercedes she had now ditched and raced inside the queen's home, the guards at the front door moving out of his way swiftly. He barged into her bedroom to find her maid hurriedly taking off her shawl and shoes. They both halted as he entered the room.

"Out!" he barked at the girl who bowed and went

scurrying from the room. He turned his attention to his wife.

"Monarch of the sky reigning on the land," she hailed calmly and curtsied.

"If you are aiming to disarm me, it won't work, my runaway Mystery Lady," he informed her in a voice that was low but held a hint of menace. "You have a lot of explaining to do."

She stood silently before him, her head bowed, her eyes to the ground, and her body trembling slightly.

"The first thing I want to know is how you, Eki Alile, the woman I repeatedly said I wanted nothing to do with, turned up at my hotel in London and seduced me. Who put you up to it? Who sent you to me in London? How did you know I would be there and at The Dorchester?" he demanded.

Eki scoffed and rolled her eyes. "Oh, please, you are about to overdose on your overinflated sense of self-importance."

His eyes widened in shock, but she was not done.

"You think I went there looking for you? It was as I told you; I sought a man to take my virginity. I never seduced you; you volunteered to be that man. What I did not tell you then and what you should know is that a major reason I wanted to be rid of my virginity was so that I wouldn't qualify to marry you. I had no desire to be your wife or queen. I wanted to be free from this hell of a life I am living. When you say you did not want to marry me, the feeling is mutual. I did not want to marry you either. Until I saw you at the Edaiken's palace, I had no idea you were the crown prince. I did not think you important enough to go looking for you on the internet. Yes, I admit it. I am not a fan! And if I had any idea who you were when I met you in London, I would have run as fast as I could in the opposite direction!"

If she had taken a knife and stabbed him in the heart, she would not have hurt him as much as her words did.

"You used me," he accused. "I thought you had

feelings for me, but you were only using me to get rid of your virginity."

"Yes, I used you! And look how that's working out for me," she laughed mirthlessly. "I used you to get rid of you, and here I am married to you and pregnant by you!"

Yes, she was pregnant. She had discovered it that morning when she had taken a pregnancy test after her late period, but this was not how she planned to tell him.

"You say that like it's a bad thing." Osad was confused. *Where was the woman who had desired him as much as he had her?* "Are you telling me that our night together meant nothing to you?"

"It meant a lot to me as long as I thought you were Owen. Once I knew you were the proud and snobbish crown prince that I sought to get away from, it meant nothing to me. Why should it? You treated me with utter disdain. Thrice you were asked to meet with me, and thrice you declined like I had some plague you were afraid of catching. In your father's study, I overheard you describe me as some local girl who could not string together words to form a coherent sentence in English. How dare you? Who do you think you are?" she demanded.

"I am king!" he snapped.

"Not to me, you are not. You are proud and arrogant; those are not the attributes of a king."

"Regardless, I am king, and your opinion is irrelevant. It is not a contest that I need to win; it is an election of birth. I was born to be king. Period!"

"Well, that is a shame because you are not fit to be king, and certainly not half the king your father was!" she spat out.

"Enough!" he bellowed. "You will speak to me respectfully or, the gods help me, I will have you incarcerated!"

She gasped in shock.

"If I was reluctant to marry you, I had good reason. Even your mother did not vote for you to be my wife. She had her doubts as to what kind of wife you would be. And do you blame me? Look at how you have handled this entire matter from throwing yourself into the arms of a total stranger to wangling your way into the palace after obviously failing the virginity test, and then not bothering to reveal your identity to me. You run around in the middle of the night going to nightclubs and bars without your husband's knowledge or consent. You are a child; an irresponsible child. You should not be left to your own devices, and you certainly should not be let out of the house without a minder!"

"I did not wangle my way into the palace!" she yelled. "I showed up for the examination as scheduled, but Usi and Edosa arrived and discharged me. I never wanted to come here. I already planned to leave Benin once the doctor pronounced me not to be a virgin and unfit for your royal mightiness!"

"I will deal with Usi and Edosa later. As for you, you will go nowhere until after my child is born. Going forward you will leave the palace grounds only when I approve it, and maids and guards will escort you. If you step out of line one more time you will cease to be queen; you will vacate these quarters and move into the harem! Do I make myself clear?"

She bowed, averting his eyes. "The crowned lion has spoken. His word is final."

He walked towards her and lifted her chin, forcing her to look into his eyes. "Good girl." He winked at her and walked away. She stood staring at him, and slowly her lips curved into a smile.

Osad was seething when he entered his quarters, and he chased out the omuadas who were waiting to serve him.

"Out!" he barked and like Eki's maid, they hurried out and left him alone.

Edosa had returned to London, and consequently, Osad could not summon him, but Usi lived less than a mile away from the palace. Osad pulled out his mobile phone and dialled his number.

"My house in twenty minutes!" he growled and hung up.

Usi must have been in the palace because he showed up in the king's residence in less than twenty minutes. Osad was standing in the middle of the Oba Olua Sitting Hall wearing a scowl. He had one hand shoved deep inside the pocket of his trousers and the other cradled a glass of brandy. He was like a leopard ready to pounce.

"You have some explaining to do, Isekhure."

"Okay." Usi swallowed nervously. "What is the matter?"

"The queen did not go through a virginity test. I understand that you cancelled it. Care to explain yourself?"

"Ah, that." Usi looked relieved. "I cancelled it because I didn't think it was necessary."

"Did you, now? Suppose I told you that she came to me without being a virgin?"

"Then I would respond by saying that if you wanted her to come to you as a virgin, you should have waited and not taken her virginity in a hotel and before your wedding night."

"Isekhure, be careful. I am not in a charitable mood, and your head is about to roll." He dropped the glass of brandy he was holding, and Usi took a step backwards.

"Forgive me, my lord."

He grunted and dropped into a sofa.

"Would you like me to call the servants to clean that up?" Usi asked, pointing to the broken glass on the marble floor.

Osad waved his hand dismissively. "Let it be. They can clean it later. I want to understand how you know about London, because I did not tell you, and even if I did, I could not have told you the woman was Eki because I did not know this until tonight. How did you discern she was the one? Did the gods reveal this to you too?"

"No. Tiyan told me," he answered. "And before you think I am a lousy chief priest, you should know that while I am blessed with the ability to see certain key events before they occur, I am unable to see events that have already transpired."

Osad nodded. "So Tiyan filled you in. I take it that this Tiyan is Eki's cousin you're currently dating?" he queried. He remembered Edosa had teased Usi about her a few times.

Usi grinned. Doubtless, he was smitten with her. "Yes," he affirmed.

"And I suppose Eki is unaware of your conversation with Tiyan?"

"Er-yes," he smiled sheepishly. "Please don't say anything," he begged.

"Go." Osad dismissed him.

Eki was asleep when she felt the mattress move beneath her. She opened her eyes and spun round in the bed.

"Osad?" she asked in disbelief as he pulled back the covers and climbed into bed next to her.

"Were you expecting someone else?" he inquired.

"No. But I didn't think you would come here."

"You don't say! Where did you think I'd go?" he teased as he pulled her into his arms and kissed her passionately.

"You do know that this changes nothing, don't you?" she challenged when he lifted his head. "I am still mad at you."

"Good. I'm mad at you too, and I meant what I said; you step out of line, and you are off to the harem."

She scoffed and pulled away, but he held her against his body, leaving her in no doubt of his desire.

"And what will I be, then, your concubine?"

"Of course not, a concubine has some dignity. You will be reduced to my love slave."

Her eyes widened in horror. "A love slave? How dare you? What world do – "

"Shut up and kiss me!" he ordered huskily. "You talk altogether too much, woman!" His lips came down on hers and silenced her. Eki moaned and deepened the kiss. Finally, he was here with her, this man that she craved so desperately. She knew without a doubt that she was his for a lifetime.

CHAPTER TWELVE

Osad opened his eyes and sighed as they fell on the clock on the bedside table. He had not expected to sleep in so late. He looked at Eki lying with her head on his left shoulder and arm around his mid rift. She appeared peaceful he would loathe to wake her. But he had a busy day ahead of him, and he was positive the omuadas were already waiting to help him get dressed for the day. He eased away from her as gently as he could, but not gently enough because she began to grumble in her sleep as soon as their bodies were parted, and then she opened her eyes, saw him, and smiled; no doubt recollecting their night of passion. He smiled in response.

"Good morning, my crowned lioness," he greeted, leaning forward and kissing her lightly on the bridge of her nose.

"Good morning, my crowned lion," she responded, gently stroking his face. "What time is it?"

"Time for me to get up," he answered. "But you can go back to sleep."

She yawned and stretched watching him as he slid on the pyjamas bottoms and tee-shirt he had discarded in a hurry upon climbing into her bed last night.

"Seen enough?" he teased, looking at her over his shoulder.

She smiled and stretched again. "Enough to carry me through the day. But I am going to have to insist on another performance tonight I'm afraid."

"Mmmm…" Osad leaned over and kissed her on the mouth. "You can always count on me to put on a good show for you, baby," he promised.

"A man who aims to please. How did I get this lucky?" she teased and was rewarded with a grin.

"By the way, I leave for America tonight. There are some loose ends I need to tie up with my business over there. I will be gone for two weeks."

"Oh. I see." Eki fought hard to keep the disappointment from her voice.

He picked her hand and held it up to his mouth for a kiss. "I want you to come with me. I thought that it would be a great time to bond away from the palace and the multitude of servants and guards and endless protocol and not to mention the press. Can you arrange to leave tonight? Our flight is scheduled to leave at 7 pm."

Eki's heart jumped for joy. He wasn't leaving her behind; he was taking her with him. He wanted her with him.

"Looks like I have been given an order and I don't have a choice," Eki feigned frustration.

"Yes," Osad said, taking the bait. "I am your king, and that is a direct order. Be ready to leave at 7 pm, woman."

They both chuckled as he exited her room through the door that led to his room. They didn't see each other during the day, but he called her in the afternoon to ask how her day was going. That pleased Eki much, and she began to think that they may well have a great marriage.

Osad was making an anonymous trip Eki noticed as they boarded Sky King with only Sato Ihaza travelling with them.

"Where are all your guards?" she asked as they took their seats.

He shrugged. "I prefer to travel light. I like to do everything light if you must know. It's not always been possible though; first I was crown prince, and now I am king, but I am one of those people who think that a crowd of bodyguards calls more attention to oneself and is more of a curse than a blessing. So, I prefer to have Sato alone with me, and he uses his discretion whether to bring in extra guards. We always have them on standby whether I am at home or abroad. But I prefer to have them as far away from me and as inconspicuous as possible."

"But what if you were attacked?" she asked, shivering at the thought.

He smiled humorously. "Sweetheart, I am Oba.

Nobody touches me. The bulletproof vehicles, bodyguards, and whatnot are just for show. No man at home or abroad can lay a finger on me. Hence, I prefer to travel light. Sato alone is usually adequate."

The stewardess appeared at that moment, forcing their conversation to a halt. "Good evening, Your Majesties," she greeted with a smile. "Would you like a drink before we take off?"

They declined, and as she disappeared further into the cabin, Eki turned to Osad, looking over her shoulder to make sure Sato was not eavesdropping. However, he had not joined them in the cabin, as he was stowing their bags.

"Was he with you at The Dorchester the night we met?" she queried in a voice slightly above a whisper.

"He was," Osad replied, causing Eki's eyes to widen as she realised that Sato had witnessed their one-night-stand.

"Was he with you at the bar?" Surely if the other man did not visit the bar with Osad, he would not know that she had been picked up at the bar like a tart.

He held her gaze and grinned as he realised why she was asking. "Yes, he was," he informed her.

"He saw us go up to your room together?" she asked horrified.

"He did indeed. He even sighted you leaving my hotel suite the morning after," he disclosed, and she groaned burying her face in her hands.

Oh, the shame. What had she been thinking?

He chuckled and whispered in her ear. "It's okay to feel some shame, Eki. You were a very naughty girl, after all."

Eki lifted her head and glared at him. She opened her mouth to say something, anything, in her defence, but he silenced her with a kiss. "It's okay. I like you when you're naughty," he teased.

Sato joined them in the cabin just then, and Osad turned his attention to him for a brief moment. "Sato, please inform the captain that we are ready for take-off when he is."

It was 3 am when Sky King touched down in JFK, and a limo was waiting to take them to Osad's penthouse in Manhattan, where his housekeeper, Mrs Odia warmly received them. She was an elderly Benin woman who had lived most of her life in America, and originally served Queen Esohe while Osad and his sisters were children.

Eki lingered to chat with the older woman who was incredibly excited to meet her and eager to congratulate her on her marriage and becoming queen. As Osad had left them to bond, it was up to the other woman to show Eki to the master bedroom once she had answered her questions about the wedding and coronation ceremonies.

To Eki's surprise, her luggage had been placed in Osad's bedroom. As she entered, he was stepping out of the bathroom wearing a towel around his hips. Eki averted her eyes feeling a little self-conscious which was silly considering that this was her husband and she had slept with him twice. Not to mention the fact that she was carrying his child.

"My things were left here," she said. It was a statement and not a question. From where she stood, she observed that her suitcases were next to his in the walk-in closet.

He shrugged. "Do you have a problem with that?"

"Er. No. I just thought that you would want me in a different room."

"No. I want you here," he assured her as he donned a pair of blue silk pyjamas bottoms. "Things are a bit different at home. Tradition and royal protocol get in the way. There is none of that here, and I see no reason why you should sleep elsewhere. Unless you are planning on escaping in the middle of the night, my runaway Mystery Lady."

"I will pretend you didn't say that Osad," she replied coolly as she moved to unpack her case.

"Take out only what you need now. Mrs O will unpack the suitcases in the morning."

"Are you sure?" Eki asked.

"Yes. I am. There's a cleaner who comes in daily so she will have help if she needs it."

"In that case then." Eki left the bags and picked up only her overnight case. "I have no problem receiving help."

Osad grinned. "I know. Your mother already advised me that you are lazy and undomesticated."

"And you went ahead and married me anyway." Eki began to walk towards the bathroom with her toiletries.

"Yes. In my defence, you had me bewitched."

"Bewitched!" she repeated pausing by the bathroom door. "How is that even possible? You hated me until you knew I was Mystery."

"Is that what you think?" Osad asked a little surprised. He squeezed past her in the doorway as he returned the towel to the bathroom. As he turned to go back into the bedroom, he pulled her up against him and kissed her. "Hate was the furthest thing from my mind even before I knew you were

255

Mystery."

"Really?" Eki probed. "And what was in your mind?"

"Lust!" he called over his shoulder as he strode towards the bed and climbed in. "Turn out the lights when you're done, will you?"

"Oh. Are you going to sleep?" Eki pouted. "I thought you would give me a bath."

He turned to look at her. "Unless that is an invitation to make love to you in the shower, which I suspect it isn't, you are going to have to manage by yourself. There are no maids here to bathe you, your royal laziness." Without another word, he rolled on his side and pulled the sheets over his body.

When Eki joined him in bed half an hour later, he stirred only to pull her into his arms, and then he was asleep again. When she woke up, it was 10 am, and Osad was long gone. Mrs Odia informed her that he had left two hours earlier.

As she was jet-lagged for the rest of that day and

the next, they didn't go out but dined at home when Osad returned from work. He appeared to be extremely busy with work because, after dinner, he left her to go into his study where he worked until the early hours of the morning when she was asleep. No matter how quietly he crept into bed he always woke her, and when he took her in his arms she went willingly, and they made love with the same passion that had been present on their first night together in London.

They quickly fell into a pattern; breaking the routine a few times when Osad invited Eki to join him for lunch in between meetings or when they dined out after his busy day at work. The more time she spent in his company, the more she found herself falling in love with him. He was everything she'd ever dreamed of in a husband. She wasn't the only one making discoveries, a week into their stay in New York, Osad admitted that he had been wrong about her and her ability to fit into his life. He had thought that as Eki lacked western education, she was a poor fit for him and his expensive western education. But being with her, discussing the challenges with his board and hearing her propose strategies he hadn't contemplated, though holding an MBA and DBA, had left him in awe.

The night he confessed he'd been wrong, he'd returned home to meet Eki in his home office on her laptop and in the middle of a video conference call. She was talking with Amenze and Tiyan about Elevate and the plan to hold their first pitch event. Osad knew nothing about Elevate, and once Eki was through he quizzed her about it, and she explained the business model, which had been her idea and he was floored. That night he had been different, the way he had spoken to her during dinner and afterwards as they watched a movie in his home theatre. Then he had been incredibly tender as he made love to her later that night, and for the first time, instead of dropping off to sleep, he had initiated a conversation.

"I am sorry," he began as they lay facing each other in the dark.

"Sorry?" she repeated, rolling over to flick the switch for the bedside lamp. "What are you sorry about?"

He gave her a rueful smile. "You know, you were right about me when you said I am not fit to be king." As she opened her mouth to protest the statement made only in anger, he put a finger to her lips and silenced her. "Hear me out," he pleaded.

Eki nodded her head, her eyes never leaving him, and he took his hand away from her mouth and cupped her cheek instead.

"I had suspected for a while that I was hasty to judge you, and tonight when you explained about your start-up, I realised that I had judged you in a hurry. When my father first spoke to me about you, all I was concerned with was status. Once I understood that your father did not fall into the league of wealthy Benin men and had been unable to give you a western education, in my arrogance, I decided that you were unsuitable, unworthy if you like, for I was that arrogant. As you know, I refused to meet you or to have anything to do with you.

When I met you in London, my prejudice and arrogance were out of the way, because you were at The Dorchester, and I promptly accepted you as being in my social class. Interestingly, after spending the night with you, I should have recognised you when I met you again in Benin. Except that the opinion I had formed of you from the onset had returned and was preventing me from seeing that you were the same woman I had accepted in London; the same woman I had wanted so much that I chose to give her my seed.

All I saw was the girl I had judged as unsuitable. Even when my body obviously recognised you and was yearning for you, I refused to open my eyes and see that the woman I sent Sato to search for was standing right there in front of me disguised only by my pride and prejudice. A good king, and a good leader, is not quick to judge those he leads and is patient and kind and willing to give his subjects a chance to prove the good in them. I never gave you that chance. I was horrible, and that's why I say you were right. I am not half the man my father was."

Eki's heart broke at his last words. She moved closer and kissed him softly. "Don't say that. I should not have said those words to you. It was cruel. Please forgive me."

"You didn't say to me that which I haven't said to myself," he replied. "I am aware that I am not a good king. I don't have the patience of my father for one thing."

"I don't think your father was always a patient man, Osad. In many ways, you are like him, and yes, that includes the arrogance and impatience. I think humility and patience came to him with age and experience, as they will to you, I am certain of it, my love."

He raised her hand to his mouth, dropping light kisses on the inside of her wrist.

"I want to go on this journey with you, Eki. I have always known that being king would be challenging and that I won't always act in the best interest of my people. Even so, I am confident that with you as my queen, I will thrive. With you, I have no fear of going astray; you have demonstrated that you are very capable of telling me exactly what you think of me and my leadership abilities."

"Oh, I remember you threatened to have me incarcerated," she reminded him, with a pout.

He chuckled. "Okay. Here's the deal. You have to observe the usual protocol when we're in public, and that includes what you say to the king and how you say it, or the council of chiefs may push for incarceration, and I may be unable to prevent it. When we're alone, though, you are talking not to your king but your husband and lover, and you won't be incarcerated. I may, however, come up with other ways to punish you for your discourtesy."

To demonstrate, he rolled her over on her back, straddled her, and fastened her hands over her head.

Eki gasped in anticipation of what was to follow. "I would like that very much," she whispered, causing him to grin.

"I know you will, shameless hussy," he whispered teasingly.

CHAPTER THIRTEEN

By the time Eki and Osad returned to Benin, anyone watching them could tell that they were in love. For one thing, they were unable to keep their hands off each other. Osad appeared to be a different man, continually seeking an excuse to come to her house or call her or pull her into his arms. He had not told her that he loved her, but his actions did it for him. He had not discussed it with her, but Eki knew he had ordered the harem cleared out upon their return and the girls had begun to vacate the house.

Consequently, Eki's fears of being replaced by another woman were quickly laid to rest. Or so she thought until the day she received an unexpected visitor, make that two unforeseen visitors, in her home.

It was evening, and Eki was at home working. Although the queen had an office in the north wing of the palace, Eki preferred to work from the smaller office inside the queen's home. She was busier than usual because Osad in keeping with his word of being a good king was setting up a bursary for Benin children to enable them to access the best of western education where they showed exceptional performance in their academics. It fell to the queen's office to manage the bursary because as he explained, it was his pet project, and he wanted her involved. In his words, it was the only way he could keep his finger on the pulse of things. She had gone to work, reporting to him when they had dinner at her residence in the evenings or breakfast in the mornings. He was spending more time in her home, only showing up at his to get dressed or undressed by the omuadas.

Today, she was lost in work and didn't realise it was already evening and Osad would soon be joining her for dinner. Apart from a couple of guards posted outside her front door, the only other person present was Yuki, who was busy with her daily tasks of cooking and cleaning. She heard voices, and looked up to see Yuki entering the room, in tow were two women; Eki's sister, Eseosa, and the other woman Eki recognised as Ede Ezomo.

"Your Majesty," Yuki began with a curtsy. "Your family are here to see you." With a bow, she removed herself from the room.

They are not my family! Eki screamed inside but held her peace.

She pushed her chair back slightly from her desk and leaned back in it.

"Eseosa, Ede," she said by way of greeting. "Please be seated. What can I do for you?"

"I like your new status, Eki, the guards, servants, fancy cars, and private jets. You're living it up. Just the way you always wanted." It was Ede who spoke first as she and Eseosa came closer to the desk and sat in two oversized leather chairs. Eki noted that neither woman observed royal protocol.

"Yes. My life is proof that if you dream enough of having a rich husband, you will end up with one," she sneered. "Be that as it may, you haven't told me how I can help you."

"Oh, I think that we are the ones that can help you," Eseosa looked at Ede, and they both giggled. "We have news that is of interest to you."

"Are you going to tell me why you are here, or shall I call the guards to escort you out? I am swamped." Eki snapped.

"Are you busy?" Eseosa scoffed, but Eki ignored her, her eyes fixed on Ede.

"Are you shopping online?" Ede nodded towards Eki's laptop. "Is that what you're busy doing?" When Eki failed to respond, she rose to her feet and signalled to Eseosa that it was time to go.

"We came to say hello and give you some news, but we will leave it to the Oba to tell you himself of our pending marriage ceremony."

Eki's heart skipped a beat. "Excuse me?" she asked.

"Osad and I are to be married. That's why I came home from America. It's all being arranged with my father as we speak," Ede said with a smile that made Eki sick to her stomach.

"You address the king by his first name?"

"Don't you?" Ede challenged. "I thought it was a privilege reserved for the women who share His Majesty's bed?"

"Please leave my home," Eki ordered. She had heard enough.

"Oh, I will go. But I will be back, someday soon when I am queen, and you are in the harem."

As they reached the door, Eseosa turned back and smiled at Eki. "Eki, beautiful Eki. You have always been able to attract the men but never able to keep them."

Right as they left, Eki's phone pinged. It was a text from Osad.

Unable to make it for dinner. I am in a meeting with Chief Ezomo, and not sure when it will end. Osad.

Osad sat in the conference room with Chief Ezomo and Chief Usi Isekhure, his eyes watching the clock. He wanted to leave the meeting and go home to his gorgeous wife. She was always a breath of fresh air and exactly what his weary soul presently longed for. He had already missed their dinner date, and he was not pleased about it. Speaking of which, he had sent her a text cancelling dinner and was yet to receive a response. He checked his phone for what must be the umpteenth time in the past half an hour. He didn't care if it looked rude, because frankly speaking, he was upset and that was putting it mildly. The truth was, the more Ezomo talked the more Osad wanted to throttle the man. The old Osad would have shut him up and thrown him out; after all, he was king. But the new man that Osad was striving to become wanted to hear him out first.

"My lord, the king, it was not your desire to marry the daughter of Chief Alile, and for obvious reasons. She is not a woman of your standing. At the time, you had no choice but to go ahead with it. But we agreed that you would put her away and marry another and I spoke to you of my daughter, who is better suited for you."

"Chief Ezomo, when His Majesty spoke of changing the rules to enable him to marry another woman other than Alile's daughter, I don't think he had your daughter in mind." Usi jumped in. "If the king wishes to put the queen away and change the rules to enable him to marry another, he will decide for himself who it is to be. You cannot force your daughter on the king. Who has heard of such a thing? You are treading on dangerous grounds, Ezomo," Usi warned.

"Stay out of this, Chief Isekhure. This matter concerns the king and me."

"As the chief priest of this kingdom, every matter that concerns the king also concerns me. The king will not marry your daughter. I do not see the king with any other woman than the queen. She was revealed, first to my father, and then to me, in dreams and visions of the night."

"If you are telling me that the gods revealed her, I will have you know that the gods are nothing but a myth." Ezomo scoffed. "I thought you would know that after years in the west, but it appears that your western education has been nothing but a waste of money!"

"You have become the proverbial dog that fails to heed its owner's voice because it is doomed for destruction," Usi warned.

"You are a fool!" Ezomo thundered. "How dare you speak to me like that?"

"You called me a fool?" Usi asked in disbelief. "Chief Ezomo, no doubt you see me as a child, but I will have you know that I am your boss. Not only am I chief priest of this kingdom, but I am also head of the council of chiefs to which you belong, and I am a kingmaker and lest I forget the mouthpiece of the gods. You are suspended with immediate effect."

"What did you say?" he turned and looked in the direction of Osad who had remained silent. "Your

Majesty – " he began, and Osad cut him short.

"Chief Ezomo, the chief priest has dismissed you. Why are you still here?" he queried. As Chief Ezomo stood to leave, he went on, "And one more thing, Ezomo, you will apologise first to the chief priest and subsequently to me for your behaviour here today, and you will do so within 24 hours, or I will change your suspension to expulsion. I am my father's son in looks but make no mistake; I am not my father. And if you attempt to cross me in any way remotely resembling the way you crossed my father, I will deal with you decisively."

Chief Ezomo who remained in shock, turned and bowed. "My lord, the king, you are a god of the sky reigning on land." On that note, he went out from the king's presence.

"The gods are a myth, and yet he refers to you as sky god?" Usi mocked.

"Will you let it go?" Osad ordered with a heavy sigh. "You have made your point, plus I let you suspend him. I don't want to hear another word.

Sometimes the way you leap to Eki's defence one wonders if it isn't Tiyan talking."

Usi laughed but did not respond, which did not surprise Osad because they both knew he was right. Usi had become like a puppy dog where Tiyan was concerned. When he was not in the palace or managing his business affairs, he was wooing her and doing everything he possibly could to please her. Osad sometimes thought he had become that way with Eki; always wanting to be with her, and please her. It was like he lived for her smile and approval. Sometimes, it scared him how much power she was starting to have over him.

Once they had returned from America, he had sent the girls in the harem packing, Ezomo's daughter inclusive, which had sparked off this evening's meeting. Ezomo thought the harem should remain as it meant his daughter stood a chance of being selected by Osad. He had asked her to return from America and was not best pleased that she had been rejected. None of the chiefs was delighted with his decision to shut down the harem. But Osad refused to allow their displeasure to sway him. It was not right to keep the girls when he had no intention of marrying them. He had not once visited any of them at night his body desiring one woman only. Besides, he didn't want Eki feeling threatened that he would take a mistress or concubine.

Like his father before him, he was a one-woman man. His father had loved his mother during her lifetime and had not taken another wife, mistress, or concubine. After his mother's death, his father had several concubines, and Osad reckoned it was his way of dealing with the vacuum his wife's death had created. Osad didn't want another woman, and whatever discussions he had had with Ezomo, unknown to the man, Mystery was the reason he sought to change the rules after he became king. And once he knew Eki was Mystery, there was no going back for him. He had no reason to consider another woman, not when she was his soulmate and the love of his life.

He wondered why she had not responded to his text message. It was unusual for her not to respond. Little did he realise that was only the beginning of unusual occurrences. When he attempted to go to her bedroom through the secret passage, the door was locked. He was weary and frustrated from the day's activities, and he wanted his bed. He would have returned to his residence, but it was starting to feel like a place where the omuadas helped him dress and undress. His bed no longer felt comfortable, and he had no desire to sleep in it.

Why had she locked the door?

If he had not been suspicious when he had received no reply to his text earlier on, he was very wary now. There was a second secret passage that linked his main reception room to hers, and he used that route. Fortunately, it was unlocked.

When he entered her bedroom, she was dressed in a silk nightgown and about to climb into bed. She gasped in shock and froze. Her guilty look was all the confirmation he needed that she had locked him out.

He was furious.

"How dare you disrespect me by locking me out of your bedroom?" he demanded striding towards her.

She spun and faced him with a wave of anger to match his. "And how dare you disrespect me by sending your lover to pay me a visit?"

Osad frowned. "What the hell are you talking about?"

"Ede Ezomo!" Eki yelled in anger. "She was here to see me this evening to inform me of your pending nuptials. The same matter you were discussing with her father. If you want to marry her, that is fine but if you think I will relocate to the harem to be your concubine or love slave while she takes over as queen you are mistaken. If you don't want me, Osad, I am gone; gone to be another's wife."

"Over my dead body!" he snarled. "I don't know what Ezomo's lunatic of a daughter told you and I will not refute it. But if that is your reason for acting up and locking me out of your bedroom, you have a lot to learn regarding our relationship. Firstly, I am king, and I need not answer to you or anyone. Do you understand?"

Eki scoffed. "You must answer to someone. Surely you are answerable to the gods?"

"But baby, I am the gods," he sneered. When she failed to respond, he went on. "Secondly, you are going nowhere. Not today, not when you have my child, not ever. If I desire that you move to the harem that is where you will go and if I desire that you serve me in the capacity of a concubine or love slave, then that is exactly what you will do. You are mine, Eki. Don't ever forget it."

"You may have my body. But that is all you will ever get from me." She glared at him in defiance.

"Oh. That is more than enough, dear Eki," he retorted, walking towards the door leading to the secret passage. He no longer desired to be with her and wanted his bed.

What a day!

He would have the heads of Ezomo and his daughter together on a platter.

As he opened the door, he turned to her. "Do not ever lock me out again, or you will not like the consequences. I was raised in the west but make no mistake I am nonetheless capable of being the African king I was born to be. That king does not care how many women have burned their bras; you are not at liberty to do as you please unless of course, it pleases him. Remember that.

Now, I will go to the harem. I am sure some girl will be happy to have me in her bed since my wife isn't. The only problem is once I touch her another can't. Thus, I will have to keep her as a concubine or maybe even a second wife."

He left without a backward glance, and as he shut the door, he heard her weeping uncontrollably. He leaned against the door and debated with himself whether to go to his bedroom or return to her.

If I go to my bedroom to sleep, she'll never believe I didn't go to the harem.

What does it matter? Let her believe what she likes. You are king, and you can do anything you want.

Yes. But she'll shut me out, and I couldn't bear it.

You can have any other woman in her stead, as many as you want.

But I only want Eki.

You must control your desire. This kind of yearning can only be destructive. You'll empower her to disregard you going forward. Go to bed and let her be. Let her think you went to the harem.

But I can't stand to hear her cry.

Then don't stand outside her door. Go to your room. From there, you'll be unable to hear her cry.

Osad paced the secret passage, and eventually, he gave in and went to her. Title and position be damned. Right now, he wanted to be with her, to hold her, and assure her that he was hers every bit as much as she was his.

He opened the door and re-entered her room. She was lying across the bed, crying her eyes out. She did not look up or acknowledge his presence as he entered. It wrenched his heart to watch.

What had he reduced his playful wife to?

"Baby. I'm sorry." The words were out before he considered what he was going to say. He paused in shock.

Sorry?

Before Eki, apologies had not come easy for him, he did not apologise to anyone, and this would be the second time in a fortnight that he was telling this woman that he was sorry.

You are fast becoming another man, Oba Ehigie. She is changing you.

That was undoubtedly a good thing. No leader was perfect; followers knew it and respected leaders more when they fessed up to their shortcomings and apologised for them.

He sat on the bed, pulling her onto his laps, and wrapping his arms around her. He had not intended to do more than hold her while she cried, but suddenly she was kissing him, and they were tearing each other's clothes off, amid a newfound passion in which their bodies said everything that their lips were unable to form.

As Eki drifted off to sleep much later, she sighed in contentment; her arms were wrapped around her husband, and she held him as though her life depended on it.

"I love you," she whispered.

"And I love you, my queen," he replied and tightened his hold on her.

She was his, and he would never let her go.

CHAPTER FOURTEEN

The following day Eki woke up before dawn and would have extricated herself from Osad's embrace but he tightened his hold.

"Thinking of running away?" he teased as his eyes fluttered open.

"Yes. I am going to run on the treadmill for an hour and take a shower. And you should return to your rooms to get ready for the day."

"I know. But first I want to talk about last night. Tell me what Ede Ezomo was doing here and what exactly she said to you."

Eki told him. When she was done, Osad groaned. "Ezomo, why do you cross lines that you shouldn't cross?" he asked of no one in particular. Then he shifted, so he was lying on his side and facing Eki.

"Eki, I will not chastise your sister or Ede Ezomo. They disrespected you in your home, and you must decide how best to reprimand them. You are the queen."

"Yes, and no one takes me seriously," she jeered.

He grimaced. "I never heard my mother say that. I am sorry if the disdain with which I treated you before our marriage and in the early days has exposed you to this sort of denigrate treatment but let me disabuse your mind if you think you are not to be taken seriously as queen. A queen is accorded the same reverence as her husband, the king. And whatever is done against the queen is done against the king.

For this reason, I will punish Ezomo, but his daughter and your sister are yours to handle. One lesson I learnt while growing up is that when a queen has her husband's ears the way you have mine, she is taken very seriously. Besides, if you can demand to drive the king's car contrary to his instructions and lock him out of your bedroom, I dare say that you are to be taken quite seriously," he joked, and Eki playfully punched him in the arm.

Later that afternoon, Eki visited her parents in their home. It was her first visit home since she'd married Osad. It was also the first time she was not going out incognito. This visit was to establish her position as queen, and it would not do to travel incognito. Earlier that morning, she had asked her assistant to inform her family that she would be meeting with them. The invitees consisted of her crew; Aiai, Tiyan and Amenze, and her parents and Eseosa. Shortly before leaving home, she had received word from her assistant that every person invited to the meeting had arrived. As was the protocol when she or Osad went out in their capacity as Oloi or Oba, guards would be deployed to the site ahead of their arrival to secure the terrain. And all guests had to be seated before the king and or queen arrived. She drove her brand-new Rolls Royce Cullinan with the specialised Oloi number plates that Osad had ordered along with the car.

After her conversation with Osad earlier that morning, she had decided on how to deal with Eseosa and Ede. However, she felt the need to tackle her sister first before confronting Ede. It was the first time she would leave the palace with guards and maids. Neither she nor Osad liked to travel heavy, and Osad had once said it was all for show as he believed himself to be untouchable, but Eki needed to put on an exhibition today. This visit was all for show, after all. She was establishing her place as an esteemed queen, and she had to arrive in all her glory as Oloi. And she did, much to the delight of her mother.

Ayi Alile was beside herself with excitement as Eki's entourage of four cars pulled up in front of the Alile residence. There were four maids, including Yuki in her convoy, and they travelled in the car behind hers. As the cars came to a halt, they exited their vehicles and stood by hers. The guards in her convoy teamed with those on the ground; together, they scanned the streets and house once more. Confident there was no danger, they signalled to the maids that it was safe for the queen to exit her vehicle. As Eki climbed out, the maids assembled around her, checking that her hair and dress were not dishevelled after the drive. Satisfied with her appearance, they flanked her and escorted her through the gates. Ayi watched it all beaming with pride. As Eki came closer, she embraced her.

"*Obo khiàn ovbi'mwen.* You are welcome, my child. I don't need to ask how you are because you look well."

Eki smiled. "Thank you, Mother." And she allowed Ayi to lead her inside. The maids hung back as did the guards and one stood barring the front door to ward off uninvited guests, and Yuki joined him, wanting to be close by if Eki needed her.

Her father rose to greet her as she entered the living room, followed closely behind by her mother.

"Ekinadoese, my beautiful daughter, you look well. Marriage suits you," he said as he drew her into his arms.

"Thank you, Dad," Eki responded. Yes, she did

feel that marriage suited her and not merely marriage but marriage to her soulmate and the love of her life. She and Osad were so right for each other.

"Hello, Your Majesty." Amenze rose to hug her.

"None of that from you," Eki laughed and embraced her dear friend. She found it hard to believe that she had not seen her in more than two weeks, although they did catch up daily via phone calls and video conferences.

Aiai was the next to embrace her. "It's so good to see you again, sweetie." She squeezed Eki until she winced, and they both laughed.

She turned to Tiyan. "Mrs Isekhure, are you going to say hello?" She joked, causing everybody present to laugh. It was no longer a secret that Tiyan and Usi were dating.

"Of course, my Oloi, I would not dare do otherwise!" Tiyan playfully retorted as she embraced and kissed Eki.

By the time Eki was seated, her mother was

already serving refreshments, and if she noticed that Eseosa had not said hello to Eki, she did not mention it, and Eki did not call her attention to it.

There was light meaningless chatter as they ate and drank, and afterwards, Eki set aside her empty drinking glass and addressed her mother.

"This is a speedy visit, Mother," she explained. "I must get back to the palace before my husband requests my presence."

"Oh, of course," her mother said with a slight frown on her face. It was clear that she did not want to offend her son-in-law by keeping her daughter too long, but at the same time, she was eager to know why Eki had summoned them.

"Eki, you asked for us to be gathered. Is there a problem? Why have you come?" her father asked, voicing her mother's concerns.

"Father, Mother, I came here for two reasons. The first is to inform you that henceforth Eseosa is banned from the palace. If she is found there, she will be detained by the guards. The second reason for my visit is to ask you to caution her. I am a queen, and if Eseosa fails to adhere to the royal protocol in her dealings with me, she will be treated as an enemy of the Oba. For indeed, what is done against the Oloi is done against the Oba."

Eki paused to allow her words to sink in. The room was silent as the eyes of all present were fixed on Eseosa who shifted uncomfortably in her seat.

"Ekinadoese, please, she is your sister. Show her mercy," her mother began, looking from one daughter to the other in dismay.

"Eki, what exactly is going on?" her father inquired.

Eki went over the previous day's incidence for the second time that day, leaving out no detail. When she was done, Ayi's mouth was hanging open. She looked around the room, her eyes darting from her husband to Aiai, Eki, Tiyan and Amenze before finally resting on Eseosa, who was squirming in her seat.

"You ungrateful child!" Ayi thundered, shocking

all present as no one had guessed her reaction would be so fierce. "Is this your plan? After everything I have done to ensure you marry well, your payback is to plot with your mother-in-law, Mrs Ezomo, to steal my exalted position as Oloi's mother? Do you ever consider the consequences of your actions? Mrs Ezomo's daughter is fit to be in the queen's house, and my daughter should be relegated to the harem as a concubine? Are you insane? Do you want to destroy this family? *Iran mu we rhia?*"

Eki exchanged glances with Aiai, Tiyan and Amenze, and they all smiled knowingly. Zogie rose to his feet and approached his wife.

"Ayi, I think you need to calm down," he cautioned her.

Ayi sprang to her feet and faced him. "No! I will not calm down. Please let me be Chief Alile!" she snapped at him and spun on her heels to glower at Eseosa.

"You are evil. You want to join hands with outsiders to destroy this family. I will not let it happen. I have shielded you enough, but this time I will rebuke you. When your sister went abroad to study, you practically moved in with Odaro. I permitted it because I reckoned that if Eki was destined to be Oloi and Oba Edoni had sponsored her education abroad, she did not need Odaro any longer. But Odaro was not enough for you, you also had your sights on Aisosa's husband, and although I was shocked when she reported your behaviour, I defended you and advised her to stop travelling around the world and mind her home. You soon became pregnant by Odaro, and we as parents plotted against our daughter to marry you off to her fiancé behind her back. When she complained, we reproved her. Have we not done enough? What more do you want? Why would you plot with Ede Ezomo to take my daughter's place as queen? Listen to me, I am Oloi's mother, and neither you nor your in-laws can take that away from me!"

Everyone watched in silence as Ayi berated Eseosa who sat there sniffling with her head bowed. Chief Alile stood between mother and daughter as he did his best to soothe Ayi, but apparently, she'd had enough of Eseosa's behaviour and refused to be quieted. As the shouting persisted, Aiai leaned closer and whispered in Eki's ear.

"You evil schemer. Look how you've turned the mother against the poor child."

"Ah, yes," Eki answered with a mischievous glint in her eyes. "It is proof that I can be my mother's daughter when it suits me."

They both laughed.

The next person to be dealt with was Ede, and that was easy. Eki learnt from her staff that the young woman was on the palace grounds and currently occupying one of the guest houses in the same wing as the harem. Although Osad had asked that the girls vacate the harem and return to their families, the moving process was slow, and many girls remained. While Eki understood that many were unable to leave the harem right away and was happy to let them stay until they could, she was unwilling to extend any such courtesy or hospitality to Ede. Therefore, when they returned to the palace, Eki led her convoy in the direction of the harem and guest houses. She pulled up in front of the guest house Ede occupied and sat in her vehicle while the guards and maids vacated their vehicles and awaited her instructions.

Yuki approached her, and Eki lowered the window to speak to the young girl.

"Yuki, tell the guards that I want Miss Ezomo and her belongings out of that house in five minutes."

She raised her window and watched as Yuki instructed the guards. They went to work straight away, and in five minutes, Ede Ezomo was standing in front of the guest house under the sweltering 30°degrees heat. Her belongings were carelessly strewn at her feet.

Eki lowered her window once again as she waited calmly for Ede's reaction. The other woman averted her eyes and curtsied. "Good afternoon, Your Majesty."

Eki ignored the greeting. "You have been a guest

in my home enjoying my hospitality, and scheming to steal my husband, but it wasn't enough for you. You had to come to my home and insult me. Consequently, I am expelling you with strict orders that you are never again to set foot in the Oba's palace during my reign as Oloi." She glanced at the guards who were standing by Ede. "You will escort her to the west gate from where I am sure her father will send a car to pick her up. If I see her within the four walls of the palace again, you will be held responsible, so be sure to pass the message to all the palace guards."

The guards bowed. "It shall be done as Your Majesty wishes," they chorused.

Before she drove off, Eki could not resist taunting Ede one more time. "Go back to America and find yourself a husband, Ede. The crowned lion sleeps in one bed only, and that bed is mine. Have a good day."

She drove home, feeling pleased with herself. No more would she tolerate any threats to her marriage.

If any chief dared to bring his daughter near her husband, she would be sure to roar like the lioness she was becoming. Oba Ehigie was hers, and she was his.

When Osad joined Eki in bed that night, they swapped stories from their day. He had expelled Chief Ezomo, and Eki was excited and mentioned that she had the perfect candidate to replace the older man.

Osad raised a brow as he stretched out beside her. "Are you appointing chiefs now, Eki?" he teased.

She raised her chin in mock defiance. "Yes, I am. I think you should consider replacing Ezomo with Efe Inneh."

Osad was silent for a while, as he contemplated her proposal, with a slight frown on his face.

"Is this what you want?" he asked after a while.

"Yes. I think it would be wonderful to have his wisdom and expertise in your council. Besides, you need to begin considering a council made up of younger men whose ages are close to yours and who have similar views."

"True," he conceded. "As long as he is happy to be appointed chief, I don't see why he shouldn't be. After all, he is Oloi's brother-in-law."

"Exactly," Eki replied gleefully. She couldn't wait to tell Aiai, knowing that she would be thrilled and so would Efe. "Thank you."

In response, Osad pulled her into his arms and held her, dropping a kiss on her head. "Do you see how influential you are? In one day, you have removed one of the wealthiest men in this kingdom from being chief and appointed a replacement for him."

Eki giggled, causing Osad to smile.

"Well done, Eki. You have truly established yourself as Oloi." He added.

Eki beamed. "Yes, I do believe I have."

He lifted her chin. "Look at me." He ordered, and she obeyed. "Do you remember what I said to you the first time I made love to you?"

She frowned. "You said many things that night."

"True. But I continually said that you are mine. And while that is true, it is only a half-truth. The whole truth is that you are mine and I am yours." He opened his hand and revealed a red velvet box from which he removed a diamond eternity ring. "I was keeping this to give to you on the birth of our child, but I changed my mind and decided to give it to you tonight." As he slipped the ring onto her finger, over her wedding and engagement bands, he declared. "I am yours, Eki. All I am and all I have is yours. I want you to remember that whenever you see this ring on your finger."

Eki was sure life with Osad couldn't get any better. She recalled how she had loathed the thought of becoming queen and living a regimented life, but life with Osad was far from regimented. He knew Eki was not cut out for the humdrum of palace life, so he frequently took her away on surprise trips and kept their marriage interesting. Eki especially enjoyed going to Lagos with him a fortnight following the incident with her sister and Ede Ezomo. They were attending a Halloween party organised by Oba Akran of Lagos.

Eki thought it was the perfect opportunity to create a new alter ego, and she did. When she had looked in the mirror, she was satisfied with the result. Even Yuki thought the new attire was better and said as much. It comprised a shimmering purple minidress set off with a halter strap that plunged into a deep neckline, finished at the cinched waist, and then fell into a gathered, asymmetrical hem. It combined well with a dark purple sparkly floor-length hooded cape made from plush velvet and secured with a single hook-and-eye fastening at the neckline.

To complete the attire, she donned a 22" straight

hair wig with full bangs, and Yuki had gone to town adorning the skin around her eyes with a purple spray paint makeup creating the perfect eye mask. With her feet clad in a pair of purple Marco De Vincenzo braided satin pumps, she was ready to go.

Osad was waiting in a white Mercedes Benz limousine outside her house. Sato met her at her front door and led her to the car. He held the door open as she climbed into the back seat, after which he joined the driver in front. Eki noticed that the privacy screen was up affording them some privacy. She also observed that Osad, who had ditched his traditional attire in favour of a two-piece dinner suit, was wearing the Anonymous mask. She caught her breath in amazement.

"Anonymous."

"Who are you?" he inquired. "I was expecting Mystery."

"Mystery couldn't make it."

"So I see."

"But she asked me to take care of you," Eki spoke slowly and flirtatiously.

"Did she now?" he asked, playing along. "And what is your name?"

She shrugged. "You may call me Misguided."

"Hmmm…. Misguided, that outfit…." he commented eyeing her long slim legs that had become visible where her cape parted.

"You like it?" she asked before he could finish.

"I do indeed, very much." As he spoke, he ran his hand up her legs and thighs coming close to the hem of the dress where he hesitated and took off his mask. "This dress is too short, Eki."

Eki sighed and rolled her eyes. "Gee, thanks for ruining my fantasy," she said dryly.

He ignored her as his eyes and hands ran the length of her legs. "When we get to that party, I want you to keep your cape wrapped around you, whether you are standing or sitting, or I will find a stapler and staple the damned thing close. I don't want other men gawking at what's mine. These are mine, to view and touch," he stated, running his hands over her thighs and up her skirt. Eki caught her breath, and he smiled, withdrew his hands, and touched her lips. "And this is for the pleasure of my mouth." He bent his head and kissed her.

They arrived at the airport, where Sky King was on the tarmac waiting for them. Once they were airborne, Osad rose, pulled her out of her seat and ushered her to the master suite at the back of the plane.

Eki giggled. "What are you doing?"

"Making sure you understand I meant it when I said to keep your cape closed and your legs and thighs covered."

He pushed her gently into the bedroom and shut the door behind them.

Half an hour later, they were back in their seats and fastened their seatbelts in preparation for landing. He looked at her.

"Who owns you?" he asked.

"You," she smiled.

He nodded. "Good. Remember that and keep that cape closed at all times."

Eki's eyes lit up as she reminisced about their time in the master suite only moments earlier.

"Who owns you?" she asked cheekily.

He leaned in and held her chin, so he was staring intently into her eyes. "You own me, my Oloi, all of me," he said and kissed her.

EPILOGUE

Six months later, a visibly pregnant Eki struggled to polish her toenails and sat back in utter frustration. It was totally hopeless. Her belly was in the way. She could not wear her strappy sandals any more than she could fix the nail polish she had smudged in an initial failed attempt to don the sandals. She now wished she had asked her maid to stay back and help her wear her sandals. But it was too late for regrets as Yuki had left for her room in the staff quarters. East wing to the south wing where she lived was quite some distance, and the girl would not make it back in time to help her. Plus, Eki would loathe to bother her.

"You aren't ready to leave?" Osad expressed dismay as he walked into her bedroom and found her sitting on her vanity stool, looking exasperated.

She sighed. "I am. Nearly. I smudged my nail polish while wearing my strappy sandals. I need to polish my toenails again, and Yuki's gone for the night." She held up the polish and waved it in her hand. "H-e-l-p!"

Osad frowned and Eki smiled. He was the best husband a woman could ask for, and although he was king whenever they were alone, he was simply her husband, friend, and lover. The last six months had been sheer bliss. She had been indulged and pampered in a way that she had not thought possible. Her husband loved her, and every moment they spent together, he proved it, showering her with his undivided attention and never-ending gifts. Everything she wanted, Osad gave her.

Her family was also basking in the overflow. Her parents had received a new house befitting their status as the king's in-laws, and even though Osad refused to reveal the extent of the gifts he had bestowed on them, Eki was certain no one would ever describe her parents as poor or lower-middle-class again. Osad had kept his word and presented Efe Inneh with a chieftaincy title, and one higher than Eki had anticipated. Chief Efe Inneh now held the coveted title of Iyase of the Benin Kingdom, which made him the traditional Prime Minister. He had also become great friends with Osad and Usi, although he said Usi freaked him out by repeatedly warning him of business perils.

Eki looked on adoringly as her husband knelt before her and took the bottle of polish from her. He grumbled a bit, but Eki didn't mind. She had come to learn that on occasion Osad would be Osad and complain.

"You do realise I am king, right?" he questioned as he slipped on her sandals and proceeded to polish one toenail after the other. "Surely, such jobs should be reserved for the maids. I mean, what would my council of chiefs say if they saw me now? Their great king reduced to polishing his wife's toenails?"

Eki giggled, and he glared at her. "Don't worry, darling. I won't tell anyone. It will be our little secret."

"I should certainly hope so," he said with mock

indignation and then lifted her sandalled feet for inspection. "Better now?"

"Oh, yes, honey," Eki said a little surprised. "How come you did it so well?"

He rose and gave her a wry smile. "Let's just say that my sisters put me through hell while we were growing up, from polishing toenails to taking out hair weaves, I've been there and done that." He shrugged and helped her to her feet.

When they arrived at Usi's home, Tiyan's 25th birthday party was already in full swing. Sato and an additional guard escorted the royal couple but as usual, kept their distance and blended into the small gathering consisting of people from Usi and Tiyan's close circles. It was a great party; from the music to the food, everything was exquisite. Eki was so happy for Tiyan. If anyone deserved to be loved the way Usi loved her, it was Cousin T.

Eki recalled with a tinge of sadness the thirteen-year-old girl who had looked so lost when she came to live at their home over a decade ago, having lost her family. It was time for her to be happy again, and Eki was glad that Usi made her favourite cousin happy. Their relationship had flourished through the months, and they were already practically living together. This was fostered because Tiyan was the only "child" staying at home and Amenze Next Door was no longer next door but spending more time in London with Dimitris. Tiyan had become lonely and begun spending more time with Usi and less time at home.

How they managed to live under the same roof and not have sex was surprising, and their resolve to wait until they were married was admirable. Eki thought they were an exceptional couple. When their friends wanted to know what the future held, they asked Usi, and if they desired information on events past, Tiyan knew a little bit about everything.

Eki's friends and family were delighted to see her, as they didn't get to see her as frequently as they would like, as she juggled her duties as queen, working on Elevate, and of course, being available to her husband. She was quickly inundated with questions concerning her due date and if she knew what she was having.

Osad wanted a boy first and then a girl he could spoil. He was also confident he had planted a male child in her womb, her chauvinist husband. She, on the other hand, wasn't fussy about the baby's sex, but they had both decided to wait until the baby was born to find out. Orobosa and Edosa Aihie were in Benin and at the party. Eki could tell Orobosa was pregnant even though the other woman's pregnancy had not become as visible as hers. It seemed they would be having their babies a few months apart. As Eki chatted with the ladies over food and drinks, Osad and the guys huddled at another end of the room talking.

Osad eyed Usi as he bit his nails nervously. "What is the matter with you, Usi?" he queried. "You have been fidgeting for the last half hour, and you look like you're sweating even though the air-conditioning is on."

Usi laughed nervously. "I am going to ask Tiyan to marry me."

Osad wasn't surprised. He had seen it coming a mile off. "Congratulations. But is that why you're so nervous?"

"Exactly." Edosa Aihie joined the conversation slapping Usi on the back in a congratulatory manner. "No need to panic. Worst case scenario she'll say no," he said and laughed at his joke.

Usi glared at him. "That's not why I'm nervous," he snapped.

Osad waved Edosa off. "Pay no attention to Edosa. Tell me, what's going on?"

"Okay. I had a romantic proposal planned. I asked the servers to put the engagement ring in the chocolate fudge dessert that was to be served to Tiyan. Except now, everyone has their desert, and I have the feeling that the one with Tiyan's ring may have been given to one of the guests," he explained.

Osad instantly picked up his desert, which had

been lying untouched in front of him as he conversed with the boys.

"Are you telling me that it is likely in mine?" he asked.

"Yes. It could be in yours or mine, or anyone's." Usi responded.

"Usi, are you saying you don't know where the ring is?" Edosa asked, joining the conversation again.

Usi turned on him. "What, are you deaf?" he asked in apparent frustration causing Osad and Edosa to laugh.

"Usi. Let me rephrase Edosa's question. As the chief priest of the Benin Kingdom a man that is revered for seeing events even before they unfold and warning the king where need be, are you telling me that you don't know where Tiyan's engagement ring is as we speak?"

"I have told you; the ring could be in anyone's desert."

Osad and Edosa exchanged looks. "Hmm,"

Edosa mumbled. "The kingdom is in trouble."

"Well, if I find the ring in my dessert, I'm keeping it," Eki stated matter-of-factly.

They had been so focused on their conversation that they had not heard her approach them.

Usi turned to Osad for help. "I'm sorry, Pal. If Eki finds it in her desert, it is hers to do with as she pleases." He shrugged and pulled Eki gently into the seat next to him as she dug around in her desert.

Usi groaned and buried his head in his hands.

Somewhat unexpectedly, Tiyan shrieked in excitement as she held out an engagement ring for all to see. Usi rose to his feet, walked up to her, and kissed her. He took the ring and went down on one knee to propose to a tearful Tiyan.

"Look at what she has reduced him to; the chief priest of the Benin Kingdom dropping down on one knee before a woman. Ugh!" Osad feigned disgust.

Eki turned to look at him in surprise. If she didn't know better, she would have taken him seriously.

But she knew better. This was the same man who brought her breakfast in bed not because there were no maids, but because he wanted to. Not to mention, he had knelt before her to polish her nails.

His eyes narrowed as he watched her, and he put his arm around her neck, pulling her in for a kiss. "I know what you're thinking. Do not even dream of saying it," he whispered against her mouth, and they both chuckled.

"Now, that's the husband I know and love."

ABOUT ETURUVIE EREBOR

British by birth and Nigerian by descent, Eturuvie 'Evie' Erebor is an inspirational and self-growth speaker, writer, publisher, talk show host, and aspiring lawyer. She has written twenty-two books and published her article series, 'Preparing to Cleave', on the Vanguard Newspaper's Christian page in Nigeria between 2004 and 2007. Her articles have also been published in various newsletters and magazines, as well as on FaithWriters.Com.

Since 2004, she's spoken in churches and schools, transforming the lives of women and youth. She has inspired and helped them realise, maximise, and fulfil their potential and destiny, and wants to continue across the world. Due to personal experience, she's determined to add more value to the lives of her fellow women. Hence, she began her initiative, 'DOZ Network'—writing and publishing DOZ Magazine, DOZ Devotional, and DOZ Chronicles as well as hosting DOZ Show and DOZ Live

Inspirational Conference.

A passionate storyteller, she's currently working on stories that appeal to women who are romantics at heart, and aid in her lifelong mission to educate, inspire, and empower with everything she does.

ABOUT DOZ CHRONICLES

DOZ Magazine was created to publish the stories of women, some painful, some joyful but all inspirational. When DOZ Magazine began operations in 2009, our true stories comprised a section within the magazine. However, readers quickly grew tired of reading the stories piece by piece. They came to loathe the phrase "to be continued", so we created an independent magazine dedicated to telling our inspirational stories in their entirety in a series. This magazine was known as the DOZ (True Story) Magazine, which significantly affected readers. It went out of circulation for a few years, but due to popular demand, it returned in 2015 as DOZ Chronicles. Under this title, four novellas were published; namely, DOZ Chronicles: Kemi, DOZ Chronicles: Lara, DOZ Chronicles: Ruki, and DOZ Chronicles: Nneka. They were published under the African Women Narratives series, and each is based on actual events.

The vision of DOZ Chronicles is expanding with its first fiction novel, DOZ Chronicles: Oloi.

Printed in Great Britain
by Amazon